Baker Company

Dan McMartin

CONTENTS

This book was originally published as a serial in four episodes.
That format is presented here unchanged.

EPISODE 1 - DAY OF DAYS

I never thought I'd say it, but I was happy to be on the old vomit comet and finally over the English Channel. After years of training, months of rumors and days of waiting, we were doing it. We were finally taking the fight to Hitler. I'm Private Antonio Giordano of the 101st Airborne Division. Me and the rest of these suckers flying over the Channel in this goony bird were part of B Company of the 506th Parachute Infantry Regiment. We just called ourselves Baker Company.

The weather that grounded us the night before had broken. The clouds, rain and heavy seas were tolerable and on the night of June 5th, 1944 we found ourselves headed for France. It was torture having the invasion called off the day before, but in a way it was a relief. As badly as I wanted to go, I was glad I'd see at least one more day on earth. I knew that there was no guarantee I'd make it through this. There was no guarantee this whole thing would even work.

I guess we were about to find out, however. Here I was on a rickety plane surrounded by eighteen others from Baker Company. Sarge had gone over the plan before boarding. We were to jump behind Utah Beach, link up

1

with other sticks and clear obstacles around Causeway 2. It might have been a great plan but it didn't work out that cleanly for most of the 101st, or the rest of the parachute and glider units for that matter.

Even so, the 101st did what they needed on D-Day. My stick wasn't so fortunate, however. We approached the coast of France and the C-47s ahead of us began taking anti-aircraft fire. I had a perfect view in the last seat right across from the open cargo door I would soon throw myself out of. We flew right into the middle of it and for the first time, I understood the chaos of war. Suddenly all the carefully laid plans were out the window as our pilots tried to avoid the flak and keep us on course.

The sky was full of explosions as the other birds pitched and dodged the fire. I saw one plane get hit and go down as its wing buckled. Suddenly, I wasn't so sure I was glad to be off the ground. The light next to the cargo door went red and as Sarge gave us the command, we all stood and hooked to the line and began our checks. I would be the second man out the door right behind Sarge. The plane pitched and rolled, men were thrown about and suddenly the whole interior was filled with a blinding orange light and a deafening explosion.

The plane shuddered as the pilot fought to regain control. The damaged transport nosed down and for a moment, I thought we were going to crash. The pilot managed to get us under control again but we no longer pitched and rolled to avoid the flak. Where the fuck was the green light? I wanted to get the hell out of that fucking plane. I'd gladly face a whole regiment of Krauts if it meant I could get my feet back on the ground. We flew for what seemed like an eternity, other planes having long since dropped their paratroopers. Then I heard it.

"The fucking pilot's out!" someone called from the front of the plane. I could barely hear it above the roar of the engines.

"Damn it! Go, go, go!" Sarge yelled. Sarge turned and

jumped and I was right on his tail. I was really ready to go now and I didn't have a second thought. As I jumped, the plane was struck again. This time the plane lurched and began to roll. I heard screams for a moment until the rush of air drowned them out. I felt the sudden tug on my harness and was jerked upright only to see the transport turning on its side, one wing threatening to buckle and a hole ripped in the cockpit. Four men that I saw made it out behind me.

I looked on in horror as the plane rolled onto its side and hurtled towards the ground. One more canopy opened behind the plane. The wounded bird, whining in protest, slammed into the earth and exploded below. I couldn't help but watch as it burned until it disappeared behind a line of trees as I floated towards the ground. I'd only seen six canopies counting mine. There were over a dozen men who probably never made it out.

The ground loomed close and I hit and rolled just as they'd taught me. I guess it was second nature now. I wasn't thinking about it. I was still thinking about those men, my friends, who never made it out. I shook it off as my chute settled onto the grass of the pasture. My training took over. I unhooked and began getting my gear in order. Cowboy found me moments later and then we rounded up Gene.

"Holy fuck! How many got out of that thing?" Gene asked. Cowboy was right behind me and Gene was right behind him.

"I saw seven counting me," I told him.

"Seven? Fuck! We'd better find the others. Let's hope you're wrong," Gene told us. We didn't take three steps before Gene motioned for us to get down. We dropped into a crouch and after a moment, I saw what he had. A Kraut patrol, three men, was headed right for us. Another three were walking the tree line off to our left. Before Gene, Cowboy and I could react, we heard one of the Germans near the tree line call out.

Four figures, the others that made it out of the C-47 I assumed, ambushed the Kraut patrol fighting them hand to hand. The three Germans that were headed our way turned to lend assistance. I could see they had their rifles ready, but they couldn't fire on the fighting men for fear of hitting their own soldiers. They obviously didn't know we were just yards away and Gene whispered harshly, "Take 'em!"

All three of us shouldered our weapons, Cowboy and I opening up with our rifles while Gene fired short bursts from his Tommy gun. The Krauts went down as they ran. Gene motioned for Cowboy and me to follow. We crept towards the fallen Krauts warily but they lay dead in the high grass. Then we heard a single shot and a scream. Gene stood and ran towards the skirmish as Cowboy and I followed.

"Flash!" a voice came from a man who rose to challenge us with a distinctive accent that told me we'd found Jimmy.

"Thunder. It's Gene," came the reply.

"They got Sarge. The fucking Kraut must've pulled his weapon as Sarge fought with him. I killed the son of a bitch with my knife, but Sarge took one in the leg," Jimmy explained. Gene was already looking him over. Gene wasn't a medic, but he'd attended a couple of years a medical school and he was all we had.

"Who's with you?" I asked, gesturing at the other two men kneeling next to Sarge.

"Bull and Ozzy. Are you guys it? I saw seven of us, but I could've missed some," Jimmy said. James Gonzales was from the Central Valley of California and had a diluted Mexican accent. His family was third generation immigrants but he still spoke like he was born in Mexico.

"That's what I counted. I think we're it," I replied and Jimmy shook his head. Ozzy, who was hovering over Sarge turned to us and ordered, "Quit fucking around. Spread out and keep your eyes peeled." Jimmy, Cowboy and I took up defensive positions around the others as they looked after Sarge. He grunted and thrashed until Gene stuck him with morphine and then he was out.

"Krauts in the tree line," Cowboy hissed and we ducked low. The Germans seemed to know we were about, but not exactly where. Suddenly Ozzy crouched next to me and said, "Grab Cowboy, circle behind them and if you think you can take them do it. If not, distract them so we can get Sarge out of here. We'll head for that clearing over there," Ozzy whispered and pointed beyond the German patrol at a break in the trees.

I looked at him, nodded and got to my feet but crouched low. Cowboy had already heard and together we did as ordered as fast and as quietly as we could manage. We emerged from the trees about fifty yards behind the Krauts. I was sure they would hear us but they walked casually. They had no idea they were surrounded by handful of Americans.

Cowboy and I crept up behind them as they meandered in and out of the trees. There were only two of them. Cowboy nudged me and ran his finger across his throat. I was thinking the same thing. We pulled our knives, dropped our packs and helmets quietly and began closing ground. When we were less than five yards away one of them turned but before he could bring his rifle to bear, Cowboy tackled him. The other reacted, but too late, and I shoved my knife into his neck and twisted, dropping his lifeless form to the ground. The other German didn't have a chance against Cowboy and he lay dead in the grass as well.

We grabbed our gear and headed to the break in the trees Ozzy had indicated to meet the others. We heard noises behind us and flashlights flared to life. More Krauts had apparently found the dead soldiers. Cowboy and I ran towards the clearing as the Germans gave pursuit. Shots rang out and bullets whistled past us and rattled through the trees. Cowboy and I ducked into the trees for cover, weaving between them as we ran. A bullet hit a tree as I rushed by it and the bark exploded hitting me in the face. I never stopped running though. Suddenly, several figures rose from the grass beyond and I was sure we were dead.

"Get down!" Ozzy yelled and I'd never been so glad to hear his gruff voice. Cowboy and I hit the ground, sliding in the grass and ending up at the feet of Ozzy, Bull and Jimmy as they opened up on our pursuers. Bullets whizzed over our heads going in both directions, but the Krauts were running blind and ran right into the wall of bullets from Jimmy's M1 and the Thompsons Ozzy and Bull carried. I looked back and saw the four Krauts fall, one of their machine guns firing into the air as he did.

"You guys hit?" Ozzy asked. We weren't and told him so. "We've got to get to cover. Sarge is stable, but his leg is tore up, probably broken. We need to link up and get him a medic," Ozzy announced. Cowboy and I got up as Bull tossed Sarge over his shoulder. We ran crouched through the clearing and then down the tree line away from the pasture we'd landed in. We found a dry ditch after a few hundred yards and we took cover in it. The moon allowed us to see structures off to the west. None were lit.

"I don't know where the fuck we are. I need a couple of you to see if you can find a crossroads, a sign, anything. Bull, I need you here to carry Sarge. Tony, Cowboy, you're up again. Try not to bring any fucking Krauts back with you this time," Ozzy said. He was being serious but the order smacked of his dry sense of humor.

"Yes, sir," I replied, tapped Cowboy on the shoulder and we crawled to the edge of the ditch and rolled out. We didn't see anything and after a moment, we got to our feet and ran through the tall grass, over a small road and towards the buildings. Cowboy called out to me and we both dropped to the ground. I looked around for Krauts but didn't see anything.

"What?" I asked quietly.

"There's a signpost up ahead. You go see what it says and I'll cover you," Cowboy said in his slow western drawl. I'd rather he would have exposed himself to go read the sign but we both knew he was the better shot. If anyone was going to cover my ass, I wanted it to be Cowboy.

"Yeah, yeah," I replied, took a few calming breaths before I dashed off. I didn't see the signpost until I was only a few yards from it. Cowboy had eyes like a hawk. That wasn't just a nickname. Private Walter McLeod was a real horse-riding, six-gun packing cowboy from Nevada. In fact, he carried a Colt revolver his dad had mailed to him in England after we left Toccoa instead of a .45.

I reached the signpost and crouched next to it. I could see Krauts patrolling the little village but a long way off in the distance. After making sure it was safe, I stood and read the sign, or tried to anyway. French wasn't my strong suit. I just hoped Ozzy could match up what I think I was reading with the names on his map. I muttered the names to myself but I did recognize one of them, Carentan. According to the sign, Carentan was nine kilometers away.

That sounded about right after studying the maps and sand tables back in England. It never occurred to me the moon was on my right and the sign was pointing north instead of south. Not until I got back to Ozzy and the rest of the guys anyway. I ran back to Cowboy and then we made our way back to the ditch and dove in. Ozzy was already under his poncho with his compass, map and a flashlight ready.

"So, what'd you find?" Ozzy asked as I joined him under the poncho.

"I saw a sign. It said Carentan was nine kilometers away. I could probably pick out the other names on the map, but I don't think I can pronounce them," I told Ozzy. He seemed to have taken Sarge's place already as our leader. It made sense. He and Gene were both Corporals, but Ozzy was older and a natural leader. Oscar Jennings was a shop foreman back home in Wisconsin.

Gene was smart, but he wasn't the kind of guy you could see leading men into battle like Ozzy.

"Show me," Ozzy said and I began to scan the map. I found Carentan right away and looked around for names I'd seen on the signpost. Nothing.

"So?" Ozzy asked impatiently.

"I'm looking. I don't see any of the other names," I said.

"Well which direction was Carentan?"

"Uh...let's see...that way," I indicated and Ozzy looked at me with one eyebrow cocked.

"You sure about that?" he asked skeptically.

"Yeah, the moon was over my right shoulder. I had to turn my back to that town to read the sign. I was facing north more or...," I began to explain but I saw what Ozzy did. I looked south of Carentan and I found every name I'd seen on the sign. We weren't anywhere near the drop zone. "I'm sure. I recognize all these names from the sign."

"Fuck! That village must be Sainteny. We're ten, maybe twelve, miles from the drop zones," Ozzy said and looked at me. I saw the worry in his eyes. I knew why. We were right in the middle of where all the Krauts were supposed to be. Ozzy turned off the light, put it, the compass and the map away and we tossed the poncho aside.

"Listen up. Christopher Columbus here seems to think we're south of Carentan," Ozzy said. For a second I thought he was going to tell everyone I was wrong but it was just his wry sense of humor. "I think he's right. Hear that?" Ozzy asked of no one in particular.

"Hear what?" Bull asked.

"Exactly. No guns, no fighting, just a few bursts of eighty-eight fire but that's way off. We should be in the middle of it, but were not. We're nowhere near the drop zones. For the time being, I think we're on our own," Ozzy said. A few of us muttered to ourselves, but no one said much else.

"Problem is Sarge needs aid. We need to find somewhere to get him help and maybe even leave him there. I don't think we can count on finding a medic or an aid station out here. A farmer maybe. I don't know." Ozzy said and rubbed his jaw.

"I saw a farmhouse while Tony was reading that sign. It was off by itself. No lights," Cowboy said.

"OK, go check it out. Take Tony and Jimmy. Stay out of sight," Ozzy ordered and the three of us looked around and seeing nothing moving, Cowboy led the way. He took us down the ditch line and then towards the area we'd been earlier scouting the sign. I saw the house now a couple of hundred yards away, but just barely. The three of us approached a small stone wall and crouched behind it.

"Jimmy and I will check it out. You stay here and cover us with those eagle eyes," I told Cowboy and he nodded. Jimmy and I hopped the wall and crawled the last few yards on our bellies.

"Could be full of Krauts," Jimmy whispered.

"Only one way to find out," I observed. My heart was pounding in my chest. Would we find a house full of Germans or an old farmer and his wife? The house was dark, save for a sliver of light coming from between the drapes in an upstairs window. The drapes were probably closed to avoid attracting Allied aircraft. Those boys would hit anything that was lit up. We didn't see anything out of sorts as we approached and I had to think if this place was full of Krauts, they wouldn't be huddled inside with the lights out and no sentry.

Jimmy and I made it to the house and stood with our backs against the clapboard walls. I nodded at Jimmy and he nodded back. I went left and Jimmy went right. We met on the other side of the house and he reported seeing nothing. Still, we chose to go to the back door, thinking it might be less conspicuous. I climbed the steps onto the landing and Jimmy waited below in the shadows, his rifle pointed at the door.

I knocked quietly and waited. I didn't hear anything and after a few moments, I was about to knock again but a faint light appeared behind the heavy curtains covering the window next to the door. The knob turned and as the door opened a middle-aged man stuck his face and a lantern in the crack and uttered something in French.

"You speak English?" I asked quietly and his eyes lit up.

"So it is true! You are Americans?" The man asked.

"Yes, Airborne. We have an injured man. Can you help us?" I asked. It could have been a trap, but I didn't think so. Krauts would have likely shot us where we stood, not answered the door cautiously dressed like the locals. In any case, we needed to find a safe place for Sarge and this was all we had. I remembered that plane falling to earth in flames. We all should've been dead but we weren't. I felt like we were saved for a reason and it wasn't to die here at this farmhouse.

"Bring him to the cellar," the man told me and I motioned for Jimmy to go get the rest of the guys. I watched him go and saw him stop to tell Cowboy what was going on. The man disappeared for a moment and came back with another lantern, though only one was lit and even that was turned down low. It seemed like way too long before Jimmy returned with Bull, Sarge on his back. Ozzy and Gene were with him too. Cowboy was still on the wall watching our backs. The old man went to open the door and I slung my rifle over my shoulder to help. Ozzy and Gene held their Tommy guns pointed at the cellar doors.

We carefully swung the doors open and laid them down. The man walked down the cellar stairs before turning and saying, "Come with me." Ozzy and Gene relaxed but didn't put away their machine guns. Gene and Ozzy followed the man who turned up the flame on one lantern and hung it on a peg once he was at the bottom of the stairs. The rest of us, Cowboy included, followed.

After the old man had lit and hung the other lantern, he and I closed the doors behind us. Once we had secured them, the man turned to me and said, "I am Claude," and he extended his hand.

"Antonio, but call me Tony," I replied.

"Nice to meet you, Tony," Claude said in pretty good English but with a thick French accent. I followed Claude back into the cellar. Gene was already changing Sarge's bandages as the rest of the guys watched. Sarge was awake, but barely.

"What the fuck happened?" he asked.

"You got shot. One of those fucking Krauts got you. You'll be fine, but that leg is probably broken," Ozzy told him. Sarge looked angry more than anything.

"Well, I guess my war is over...for now anyway. Where are we? Did we link up with anyone?" Sarge asked, still trying to lead from his makeshift hospital bed.

"That's the really bad news. We're nowhere near where we should be. We're south of Carentan. Way south," Ozzy told Sarge.

"I saw the plane after I jumped," I said and everyone turned my way, "It had a gaping hole under the cockpit. I heard someone say the pilot was out."

"I heard that too. We took a big sweeping turn. Who knows how long the pilot was out of commission," Gene said.

"I thought he was making another run at the zone. If I'd have known he was dying, I'd have ordered the jump," Sarge said groggily.

"It's not your fault. You did what any of us would have done," Ozzy assured Sarge and then told him, "We're safe for the time being. Get some rest." Sarge was already asleep, however.

"I'm Corporal Oscar Jennings, but you can call me Ozzy," Ozzy said to Claude as he turned to greet the man.

"I am Claude. I am so glad to see you. So the rumors are true? You are here to liberate France?" Claude asked.

"That's the plan. This is Gene, that big guy is Bull, he's Jimmy, that one's Cowboy. I think you already know Tony," Ozzy introduced us in turn. The other guys nodded in turn. Then Claude took Ozzy's shoulders and kissed him on the cheeks, which brought a few chuckles from the guys.

"How can I help? Anything you need," Claude offered and Ozzy told him we needed a doctor. "Of course, of course. I will see what I can do. I have a friend that is a surgeon. He will be as excited to see you as I am. Do you need food?" Claude asked.

"Food would be good. We can save our rations. Thanks!" Ozzy told him. I'd have rather just lost our rations.

"I will return shortly. I will knock three times. If I do not, shoot," Clause warned and then smiled and said, "Do not worry, you will be safe for the time being." Claude went up the stairs and Bull covered the lantern at the foot of the steps until he was gone. Jimmy was already smoking a cigarette and Bull offered his pouch of tobacco to Cowboy who took a big dip and shoved it in his mouth. Neither man smoked, but they both chewed tobacco liberally. Soon we had all found a place to relax and only Gene wasn't smoking or chewing tobacco.

"Welcome to France, boys," Bull announced.

"How many fucking Krauts did we get?" Jimmy wondered.

"I think we got a dozen of the bastards," Gene said. Gene was Jewish and had no love of the Nazis. He even had family in Europe but had lost contact with them after the Germans overran the continent. He was a gentle kind of guy but he was here to kill Nazis. That's why he joined and when they told him the paratroopers would likely be the first in, he volunteered. I suppose we all had our reasons for being here but his seemed the most immediate.

"Twelve! Holy shit. Still not enough to make up for Sarge," Jimmy said.

"You got that right," Cowboy answered in his usual slow drawl.

"I guess that makes you our sergeant now, huh Ozzy?" I observed.

"Whatever you call him, he's in charge," Gene said. Gene had no desire to lead. Ozzy on the other hand, was a natural leader. He had a good head on his shoulders and inspired confidence among the men. He could be a real hard ass but he had sense of humor too.

"I suppose so, though I'd rather Sarge was still in the game," Ozzy replied.

"So what now?" Bull asked. I'm sure we were all wondering the same thing. I know I was.

"I'm not sure. We're a long way from the drop zones and I'm willing to bet there are a lot of Krauts between here and there. We can wait until the boys on the beaches break free or the Airborne gains some ground but that could be days, maybe weeks. I, for one, don't want to spend the war relaxing in this cellar while the rest of the 101st gets all the glory," Ozzy said.

"Fuck that!" Jimmy said. Jimmy talked big but tonight he backed it up. He was always saying he was going to kill a thousand Nazi's but, honestly, I would have thought he'd be the first guy to fold. He seemed to like shooting his mouth off but he did alright.

"Yeah, I'm not one for sitting around and waiting to get captured and I sure as hell don't want to be found luxuriating in some farmhouse," Bull added. Private John Tucker, Bull as we called him, was a big man. He worked on his family's farm in Oklahoma before the war and it showed. He was well over six feet tall and was wide as Jimmy and I combined.

"So, even though I'm apparently in charge, I need to know. Are you all with me? Are we going to do what we can to help? We might die. We might end up captured.

Your folks might not ever know what happened to you," Ozzy explained. He said what we already knew but hearing it was sobering. However, none of us signed up to jump out of a perfectly good airplane, that was the theory anyway, to sit around eating cheese and drinking wine until the rest of the United States Army fought their way to us.

"I'm with you, Ozzy," Gene said. We knew Bull was in and Jimmy too.

"Yup, I'm in," Cowboy added in his abrupt way. Everyone looked at me.

"I go where you guys go. You're like family. Now, if Gene could learn to cook like my mom this would be perfect," I said. Ozzy smiled.

"Good. We'll kick some Nazi ass and God willing, we'll all stay alive long enough to find our way back to the 101st," Ozzy said.

"Maybe Claude could point us in the right direction. There's got to be something we can do," Gene offered.

"We'll ask him. We're out in fucking left field here. We'll see," Ozzy said and everyone seemed to get quiet then. Dawn was coming. Time flies when you're running around France lost and scared. Cowboy was already asleep and Bull was on his way. They could sleep anywhere. Gene checked on Sarge while Jimmy simply sat and stared as he smoked his second cigarette. Ozzy offered to take watch, but I told him I couldn't sleep and I'd keep watch so he could get some shuteye.

"Thanks, kid. You did good tonight," Ozzy said as he went to find a relatively comfortable spot to sack out.

I thought about that German I'd killed while I sat alone in that cellar. I was pretty sure I'd shot at least one of the three that almost stumbled upon us in the pasture but the other one was different. I stuck my knife in his throat and took his life. He was still gurgling when I laid his body on the ground, though his eyes were already glazed over. I didn't feel bad about it, but it made me think. I could've been just like him, lying dead in some pasture.

I forced myself to think of home instead, my mom and pop, my younger brothers and my older sister. I missed them. I missed home. I wanted some of my mom's cooking desperately, maybe some lasagna or chicken parmesan. I wanted to be sharing a room with my brothers, begging my sister to get out of the bathroom and hearing my mom yelling at us to be quiet. I wanted to hear my pop bust my chops about my grades one more time.

Just then, I heard three knocks. I got up, unbarred the cellar doors and found Claude and another man, the doctor I assumed. I let them in and could see the pale light to the east. I knew the invasion was beginning, but I tried not to think about it. I didn't think about all those men coming ashore and probably dying. Instead, I said a quiet prayer that they would succeed so I might get to go home again.

"I've brought the doctor and news. Friends have told me that there have been many sightings of parachutes and American soldiers. Sadly, none nearby. Most of the sightings are much closer to the sea," Claude told us as Gene greeted the doctor and took him to check on Sarge.

"God bless all of you," the doctor said in barely recognizable English as they went.

"Any news from the beaches?" Ozzy asked as Claude finished closing the doors to the cellar.

"No, nothing," Claude answered.

"It's early yet. Will you tell us if you do hear any news?" Ozzy asked.

"Of course. I will bring breakfast. Do you need anything else?" Claude offered.

"As a matter of fact, we need something to do. We've determined we probably can't link up with the rest of our units. That doesn't mean we want to lounge around in your cellar though. No offense. We were hoping you might have some idea," Ozzy asked and I wondered what an old farmer like Claude could possibly know.

"I have already contacted friends. They are with the

resistance. They know of the invasion and would be interested in assisting you. They will come tonight if you wish," Claude said as if he'd been reading Ozzy's mind.

"We do. Who are they, how many?" Ozzy replied.

"I have spoken with only one man. He and his daughter work alongside a second man. They gather intelligence, but they belong to a larger group. I will tell them to come tonight," Claude said. More waiting, but at least we were comfortable.

The doctor did what he could for Sarge and through Claude he told us Sarge would survive. However, he would not fight again and likely walk with a limp the rest of his life. The bullet shattered the bone in Sarge's thigh. Claude told us that after dark we could move him upstairs and dress him in civilian clothes. We had little choice at the moment.

After Claude brought us pastries and milk, I slept until midday and then Cowboy, Jimmy and I played cards throughout the afternoon. Around four that afternoon, Claude told us he'd received news of the landings. Nothing specific, but American and British troops were moving inland. He also said that German units were beginning to move towards the coast.

"How do you know all this?" Gene asked after he heard the news.

"Coded messages and gossip. News such as this travels fast," he said evasively.

"Good news mostly, if it's reliable," Ozzy said.

"What about them Kraut units?" Bull asked before stuffing another wad of chewing tobacco in his mouth.

"That concerns me. The Krauts will push back and push back hard. What time will your friends be here, Claude?" Ozzy asked.

"Eight. I will bring dinner soon and water to fill your canteens," he said and disappeared again. The next four hours dragged by slowly. Most of us dozed, played cards or just wallowed in our own thoughts. Except for dinner, those hours were brutal. I think we were all ready to get moving and do something, anything, but if the other guys were like me, doubt was beginning to creep into their heads.

The longer I sat in that cellar, the more I thought about dying or being captured eventually if the invasion failed. I worried about the guys I knew in the 101st and the other men coming ashore. Without something to do, some goal or plan, it was easy to despair. I tried to focus on what might happen after we met the resistance instead. I hoped they would show soon.

As if to answer my prayers, Claude arrived moments later and with him were three others as promised. We weren't so jumpy now, used to Claude's comings and goings. The three others didn't look like I'd expected. The men looked a lot like Claude, basically farmers. The young woman, on the other hand, didn't look like a resistance fighter but she didn't look like a farmer either. She was beautiful with black hair that hung just past her shoulders, pale skin and full red lips. She wore a floral dress and heels.

"Ozzy, this is Francois, his daughter Margaux and Henry," Claude announced and Ozzy stood to greet the others.

"I'm Corporal Oscar Jennings, U.S. Army, 101st Airborne but you can call me Ozzy. Glad to meet you," he said as he shook Francois' hand and then Henry's. We'd been trained to seek out the resistance and use them to help our cause. They knew the countryside but more importantly, they had been fighting the Krauts for years. They could provide intelligence and support and they were eager to take their country back from the Nazis.

"Honored. Claude tells us you are lost?" Francois said in a thick accent.

"Not exactly lost but we're not where we should be. I don't think we can get there either," Ozzy explained.

"You are correct. Many Nazis are between you and

your compatriots. More are moving that direction as we speak," Francois said confirming what we suspected.

"In that case, we're hoping you might be able help us find something to do. These boys are looking to cause some trouble," Ozzy replied. Claude and Margaux laughed softly.

"Oui, I think we can help. We have been scouting all day. There is a column of Nazis moving north. They have several guns and maybe one hundred and fifty men. I have twelve men in addition to Henry and my daughter. We have explosives and with help we can possibly sabotage the guns. Together we may cause even more problems for the Nazis," Francois explained.

"Sounds right up our alley. Tonight?" Ozzy asked.

"Oui, tonight. Will you assist us?" Francois replied.

"Damn right we will. Tell us what you know?" Ozzy asked. He, Gene, Francois and Margaux huddled over Ozzy's map. The rest of us gathered around and listened. The column was just over a mile away and digging in for the night along the road. As with pretty much all the land around here, the pasture they had selected was surrounded by hedgerows and trees. They devised a plan that had the French providing a distraction while we spiked the guns. It was a hit and run operation. We'd do what damage we could and retreat before the Krauts could collect themselves and counterattack.

This wasn't about glory. It was about slowing down the Krauts and not taking casualties. We'd move in under cover of darkness, find and kill the sentries, use the explosives the French would provide, as well as our own, to destroy the guns. Before the Germans organized a counterattack, we'd be gone. That was the plan anyway. However, we wouldn't be returning to Claude's farmhouse. Francois indicated he could house us more securely and showed Ozzy and Gene where on the map.

It was almost 2100 hours when Francois and the others left. Francois promised he and Margaux would return before midnight to collect us. Henry, who I got the feeling didn't speak English, was to lead the French while Francois and Margaux would accompany the six men of Baker Company. Ozzy wasn't sure about Margaux going with us, but Francois assured Ozzy his daughter could hold her own. I had a hard time picturing that pretty girl in battle.

"All right, let's get ready. Make sure those rifles are clean and you've got all you're gear. We won't be back here again, so it all goes," Gene ordered after the French resistance fighters left. It felt like the night before the drop again. Excitement tempered with a healthy dose of fear. Fear of dying, fear of letting your buddies down and fear of the unknown. With time to spare, we were all geared up and ready to go. Stuff hanging from our suspenders and belts, packs full and rifles ready.

Cowboy and Bull dug into their tobacco pouches while the rest of us, except for Gene, smoked and waited nervously. Finally, the three knocks came and it was time to go. Claude opened the doors to the cellar and we all emerged. I hoped Sarge would be OK, but Claude was a good man and he'd see that Sarge was kept safe. Francois and Margaux waited. Francois looked no different, middle aged, overalls and a tattered coat.

Margaux, on the other hand, was in slacks, a sweater and jacket with ladies boots. Her hair was tied back and she wore a beret. She still looked beautiful. Both carried rifles, old bolt action models I didn't recognize, and packs on their backs. "Are your men ready?" Francois asked.

"We're ready. Lead on," Ozzy said. I looked around at my buddies. I prayed we'd all make it through the night. A few of them were doing the same. Francois and Margaux led the way and before I followed, I thanked Claude.

"You're welcome. God bless. I'll take care of your friend," he said as I turned and left him behind. We didn't hurry but instead walked quietly, only moving quickly when we were exposed. Our route took us through the trees and along hedgerows turning the mile to our objective into two or more with all the meandering amongst places we could remain concealed. We were in Nazi-occupied France but we only had one brush with the Krauts. Without immediate action and reports of paratroopers falling from the skies, the Germans in our area weren't on high alert.

We approached a road, needing to cross to get to the objective and cover on the other side. As we neared, the sound of an approaching vehicle shattered the eerie quiet and it was coming our way. The eight of us were caught in the open with nowhere to hide. Ozzy motioned for everyone to run. I expected we would go backwards, but we ran forward towards the road instead. As the car appeared around a bend, all of us managed to dive against the embankment at the side of the road. I held my breath as the car approached.

I dared not look up, but Cowboy told me later it was a German staff car. He joked that it was carrying Hitler and if he had his lasso, he'd have roped him and ended the war. I believed he could have. The car passed and I finally exhaled. I think we all did. Francois moved first and checked the road. It was clear and we proceeded. I doubt we were in any real danger. A bunch of American paratroopers this deep in France was probably the last thing the Germans were expecting.

Still, the episode made me realize how tenuous our situation was. We had no help, no one to fall back on and no relief. If we were caught or killed, no one would ever know, assuming we perished with the rest of our stick when the plane went down. That thought made this all so much more immediate. We were no longer part of a bigger war. This was our war and we were in control of our own destiny. The fact that each of us chose to do what we could to aid the larger effort instead of just waiting to be saved made me proud as hell.

We followed Francois and it wasn't long before we approached the pasture the Germans were camped in. Each of us, in twos, scouted forward to get a lay of the land. Men and tents, Germans, littered the pasture a couple of hundred yards ahead. Nearer to us, two eighty-eight millimeter guns we simply called eighty-eights each sat behind the trucks that towed them lined up just off the road. I could clearly see the sentries that watched over them. Francois explained the rest of the Maquis, the name given the resistance fighters, were in the tree line past the tents at the opposite end of the pasture. It was nearly 0100 on D-Day plus one. Yesterday we got a taste of war but today we'd get a belly full.

Ozzy went over the plan once more. We'd drop our gear, helmets, packs, everything. We'd be going in quiet and didn't need all that stuff rattling and clanging about. Gene, Cowboy and I would take the second gun. Ozzy, Bull and Jimmy would take the one ahead of it. Francois and Margaux would watch our flanks and cover our retreat if necessary. Ozzy and Gene even handed their tommy guns and several clips over to Francois and his daughter. Ozzy and Gene would be handling the explosives while we covered them so they didn't need their machine guns. Besides, the old bolt-actions rifles Francois and Margaux carried wouldn't do much good.

Cowboy, Jimmy, Bull and I would provide cover for Gene and Ozzy and keep any wandering Krauts from messing up the plan. We had ten minutes or so to get into position before the Maquis would provide us with a distraction in the form of a large frontal assault or something that the Germans would assume was a frontal assault. In reality, they'd be firing, moving and firing again to make their numbers appear larger.

After checking our gear, we carefully picked our way through the trees and around to the rear of the eighty-eights. We were nearly fifty yards away when we ran out of concealment. Francois and Margaux waited there to cover our exit as we covered half the remaining distance on our bellies in a wet ditch that paralleled the road. Lying in that ditch, we waited for the Maquis to spring their surprise. We didn't have to wait long.

A single shot rang out, then another and soon the quiet night was gone in favor of what sounded like an all-out attack. The Kraut camp erupted in chaos as the Maquis laid into them. Even from our vantage point we could see the German's desperately attempting to ascertain the situation and mount some kind of defense. Several Germans were already down dead or wounded. The Krauts returned fire and could be heard screaming and yelling in surprise and fear.

The six men of Baker Company slowly moved forward. The sentries, as we'd hoped, had turned their attention to the attack and left the guns mostly unguarded. The men sleeping near the trucks hauling the eighty-eights were up and moving towards the Maquis. As we approached the big guns, only a handful of men remained near them but their attention was on the emerging battle instead of the six men who crept up behind.

We emerged from the ditch, Ozzy, Bull and Jimmy heading for the first gun, Gene, Cowboy and I towards the second. One of the sentries who had remained behind turned but Cowboy was there, his hand over the man's mouth and his knife blade in his throat. He laid him gently on the ground as I moved on the other sentry. I crouched behind the eighty-eight and after a moment quietly crept up behind him. He never turned, the battle proving to be the distraction we'd hoped. I dropped him to the ground after opening his throat. Gene was already readying the explosives. They had a time delayed fuse and would blow after several minutes. Unfortunately, Gene never got his lit.

A Kraut yelled from a distance. He'd seen us and warned several others of our presence. Gene dropped his package down the barrel of the eighty-eight even though it wasn't lit. Cowboy killed the German soldier who had spotted us, but it was too late. Two dozen Krauts appeared and I barely made it to cover behind the big gun before they opened up on us. Bullets whizzed by and rang off the metal of the eighty-eight. I returned fire, as did Cowboy and the others pinned down behind the first gun.

"I dropped the explosives down the barrel, but I didn't light the fuse," Gene shouted as he pulled out his .45 and began returning fire.

"Grenade?" Cowboy offered.

"Not while we're using this thing as cover," Gene reminded him. The Germans were crouched in the open. Cowboy had taken down two and I was pretty sure I'd got another. The other team behind the first gun had killed one or two Germans as well. Still, we had nearly twenty enemy soldiers advancing, nowhere to go and only four rifles among the six of us. The Maquis were too far off to lend help and Francois and Margaux couldn't do much from their position behind us without exposing themselves.

Suddenly, Ozzy shouted, "Cover us!" Cowboy and I reloaded and emptied our clips at the advancing Krauts as Ozzy's team joined us, sliding in amongst us behind the second gun. The eighty-eight was a big hunk of metal but even it wasn't adequate cover for six men. We were stacked behind the available cover, taking turns firing and reloading, but it was clear we didn't have enough ammo to trade fire for long.

"Our gun's spiked. You?" Ozzy asked.

"I dropped the explosives down the barrel when these assholes showed up. I didn't light the fuse," Gene said.

"Shit! We've got a couple of minutes before ours goes off. We'll have to hold out until it blows and use the confusion to retreat. When the other gun goes off, get a grenade down the barrel of this one. That should set off the explosives," Ozzy instructed. The Krauts were within fifty yards and some of them moved to flank us around the front of the other truck. A couple of minutes was a fucking lifetime right now.

We had decent cover from either direction behind the big eighty-eighty, but taking fire from both sides would cut off our escape route. "Bull, Jimmy, move up behind the truck and toss a few pineapples their way," Ozzy ordered. Cowboy and I provided cover as they moved. The truck hooked to the big gun kept Jimmy and Bull safe from the larger group of Germans. They both readied grenades as Ozzy lay down next to the eighty-eight and watched the men trying to flank us advance. He had a clear line of sight under the big truck.

"Now!" he yelled and Bull and Jimmy tossed their grenades past the other gun and they bounced near the first truck. The half dozen Krauts lined up in front of the first truck tried to scatter but it was too late. The blasts decimated the men attempting to flank us. Two of them stumbled into the open and Bull and Jimmy shot them dead. However, more Krauts were coming to reinforce the main group advancing on us as they realized this was the real fight. Things were going from bad to worse.

The Maquis attack waned as the Germans figured out they were facing an inferior force. The biggest group of Germans was still focused on the Maquis attack, but our little party was beginning to draw more attention, including a machine gun team with an MG-42. We had a lot of open ground between us and safety and even the eighty-eight exploding wasn't going to provide us with enough of a distraction to avoid that machine gun fire.

"Cowboy, take that machine gun out," Ozzy yelled. Cowboy found them working their way up from the rear and managed a head shot on the man carrying the ammo box, but the others eluded him.

"Oz, we've got to get the fuck out of here," Gene shouted and Ozzy looked back at him. The look our leader wore told us he wasn't sure this was going to end well for any of us. We were safe for now, but those advancing Germans were eventually going to overwhelm us.

"Ozzy, this truck's fucking full of ammo," Jimmy said. Ozzy turned and suddenly he looked optimistic again. He told Bull and Jimmy to get back behind the eighty-eight with us. I provided covering fire as Bull and Jimmy joined us. Cowboy was searching for the machine gunners and found them behind a small mound as they unleashed a little bit of hell on us. Suddenly, the sound of bullets ringing off the eighty-eight took on a deeper more deadly tone.

"Everyone put a grenade in the back of that truck on my signal except you, Gene. You get one in that barrel. Then we run, down that ditch, low and fast. God, I hope those Frenchies are still waiting with those Thompsons to give us cover," Ozzy ordered. I'd almost forgotten about Francois and Margaux. I wished they were closer to help.

Suddenly, as if in answer to my wish, two tommy guns opened up from the trees behind the Krauts. Thank God for those two French freedom fighters, I thought to myself. They must have taken the initiative to move and distract the Germans. It was a good eighty yards away, but it was enough to draw the Krauts attention away from us for a moment. Ozzy shouted, "Now!" Five grenades went into the truck and then we broke from cover. Each of us with a rifle emptied our magazines into the confused Germans as we ran. Gene shoved a pineapple in the barrel of the eighty-eight.

"Go, go, go!" Gene shouted but everyone was already running along the ditch. I heard the MG-42 open up but not at us. It shredded the trees where Francois and Margaux had surprised them. As I ran, I saw as the machine gun cut the trees to pieces and I hoped and prayed they had long since vanished. I also spotted a handful of Krauts giving chase and their bullets whistled past us and threw up splashes of mud and dirt around us as we ran.

Just then the truck exploded, a series of smaller blasts from our grenades followed by a much larger one that lit up the pasture like daylight. As that explosion faded, another could be heard but it was a more of a hollow thud. At least one of the eighty-eights had been destroyed. The German's behind us continued their pursuit, firing as they did. I'd run the three miles up and the three miles down Currahee but it seemed shorter than the hundred yards we had to cover now. Then suddenly, Jimmy went down just ahead of me.

"Fuck!" he shouted. Cowboy and I grabbed him by his suspenders and dragged him along with us. Dirt flew as bullets hit the ground around us and the air seemed so full of lead that I couldn't believe Jimmy was the only one who'd been hit. I dared to look back again and the Germans were closing. Ahead we had thirty yards left to reach the relative safety of the trees. A bullet tore through the shoulder of my uniform and I felt a burning sensation. Even so, I kept running.

Time seemed to slow and like some kind of dream, the tree line seemed to move further away the further we ran. I knew this was it. We'd run out of options and even if we made the trees, the fucking Krauts would catch us. Still, I ran, dragging Jimmy, hoping against hope. Then Gene took a bullet and stumbled, but he managed to keep running. It was only a matter of time.

Then the trees ahead of us erupted with flashes of light and the sweet sound of two Thompson submachine guns. The Germans fell under the withering fire, screaming and shouting. Suddenly, we were in the trees and met by Francois and Margaux. The pursuit had stopped and the remaining Krauts were headed the other way.

"Come, we must go," Margaux said. Francois helped Bull get Jimmy onto his shoulders. I took a second to look back. The second truck was a burning heap and both eighty-eights had been destroyed. The camp was in complete disarray but now the pasture was still save the burning trucks and the angry shouts and painful cries of the German soldiers. Just a few yards away beyond the trees, most of our pursuers were dead.

We didn't waste any time, running through the trees to our hidden gear. We grabbed it, putting on what we could and dragging the rest. We broke for safety though it seemed the German pursuit had been stopped for now. However, we weren't taking any chances. A few dozen Germans lay dead but over a hundred remained and they were sure to mount a search.

We ran through the night, mostly in cover when we could manage. No one spoke, but our heavy, ragged breathing seemed loud enough to be heard for miles. Finally, Francois brought us to a halt in a heavy stand of trees. Gene seemed to be fine but Jimmy was hit badly. My shoulder hurt but I didn't feel any blood when I checked. In any case, we'd have to wait to dress our wounds.

"The safe house is just ahead in that field. Margaux will take you there. I must check on my men. I will join you in the morning," Francois told us. Ozzy thanked him and shook his hand. Francois nodded and disappeared through the trees. I looked where Francois had indicated and there was nothing there. No house, no barn, nothing, just an empty pasture.

"Come, we should get to safety before the Nazis begin searching for us," Margaux said. She moved along the trees, then a hedgerow and after a momentary search she bent and picked up two thick ropes. "I need help," she said. Cowboy and I took the ropes from her and she told us to pull them. A piece of ground lifted from among an identical patch of ground and revealed a stairway. The hatch was cleverly hidden within a copse of trees and nestled close to a hedgerow under a patch of grass growing from the earth atop a wooden frame.

Margaux ushered us inside and I helped her close the door above us. She pulled the ropes back through holes in the door where they were held with knots on the end. Margaux searched in the darkness and found a lantern, which she lit and then led us down a narrow tunnel braced with wooden planks. We walked a few dozen yards before emerging into a large room that looked much like Claude's cellar.

Bull set Jimmy down on the table in the center of the room and Gene began looking at his wound, ignoring his own. The rest of us explored the room. The walls were stone, the floor wooden planks as was the ceiling that was supported by wooden posts and joists. Roots from above had worked their way through between the planks. Shelves with food, medical supplies, weapons and ammunition along with other supplies, including wine, lined the walls and one corner housed bunks, eight in total. The table Jimmy lay on was sturdy and ornate as were the chairs surrounding it.

"This is a cellar of a house that burned before the war. This cellar survived and sat open for years but when the Nazi's invaded and the resistance was formed, a roof was built and covered with earth. The Nazi's do not know of its existence. Above us, like the door, the roof is covered in grasses and appears like any other pasture. We use this place for storage, planning and refuge," Margaux explained.

"Clever," Ozzy said.

"You may take advantage of any of the supplies. I wished we had more weapons and ammunition for you. You may need to scavenge Nazi weapons and ammo when you run out," she offered and went to help Gene. It turns out a bullet tore through the side of Jimmy's thigh, but the wound was superficial. Once Gene had patched up Jimmy, he asked Margaux to bandage him where a bullet had grazed his arm. When Gene was finished, I showed him where a bullet had grazed my shoulder and he patched me up as well.

"Anyone else hit?" Gene asked but everyone else had

escaped unscathed.

"Miracle of miracles," Ozzy observed and then added, "I can't tell you how many bullets whizzed by so close I could feel the wind." A few of us laughed though it was an uncomfortable sort of chuckle.

"Did we get the guns? I never looked back to see," Bull asked.

"We did. I saw both of them. The barrels were torn to shreds," I told him.

"That was intense. I'm sorry I fucked up," Gene said.

"It worked out and you did your job. Nothing ever works out as planned," Ozzy told him and patted Gene on the shoulder. "Settle in and get some sleep. I suspect we'll be here for a few days," Ozzy instructed and we all found a seat. Soon the room was filling with the sweet aroma of Chesterfields and Lucky Strikes. Bull and Cowboy both had lips full of chewing tobacco. Only Gene abstained. I noticed Jimmy's hands shaking as he smoked, but he seemed fine otherwise.

Margaux took a seat in the far corner by herself. I watched her until she looked up and smiled. I went to her and offered her a cigarette. She took it and thanked me in French before sliding over and offering me a seat on the crate she sat upon. I sat down and lit her cigarette with my Zippo. She took a deep drag and blew the smoke from her red lips.

"This is so good. We cannot get good cigarettes since the war began," she said and I offered her a few of my sticks. "No, you cannot get more," Margaux told me.

"I smoke too much anyway," I said. She smiled and took them, thanking me again in French.

"How is your shoulder? Does it hurt?" she asked. Damn, she was beautiful, like a movie star. Red lips, flawless skin and now I noticed her deep blue eyes.

"No, it's fine. Just grazed me," I said. It occurred to me that if that bullet had been another inch lower, I'd be out of commission or maybe dead. Same with Jimmy and

Gene and how many of the other guys had escaped by a whisker? We were lucky tonight. I wondered if the Maquis fared as well. They had taken the brunt of the German counterattack. Only the fact the Germans weren't expecting an attack made what we did possible. I doubted they would make that mistake again.

Margaux and I sat together smoking in silence. When she was finished with her cigarette, she slipped her arm into mine and laid her head on my good shoulder. I was too tired to think about it too much. All I know is it felt nice. She fell asleep a moment later. Only Ozzy and I were still awake. Ozzy looked over at me and caught my attention. He grinned at me and I shrugged my shoulders gently. He laughed softly. "Get some sleep, lover boy," he whispered.

I did eventually fall asleep. Once the excitement of the fight had left me, I could hardly keep my eyes open. It was 0600 when Francois showed up. I awoke to find Margaux already up. I joined the others to hear the news from Francois.

"How are your men?" Francois asked.

"Minor wounds. We were lucky. You?" Ozzy replied.

"Good to hear. We were not so lucky. We lost two men. Still, we did what we needed to do. The Germans took many more casualties. I've killed Germans in two wars now," Francois said. My uncle fought in The Great War too. I guess Francois did know what he was doing.

"I'm sorry for your men, Francois," Ozzy offered.

"They died heroes and will be remembered for their sacrifice," Francois said. After a moment his demeanor changed and he smiled, "I am famished. Do Americans like cheese and wine for breakfast?"

Cooking in a basement with one narrow exit wasn't a good idea. However, the cheese, cured meat and wine really hit the spot. As we all rested digesting our meal, Francois suddenly said, "I almost forgot! The invasion forces have broken out from the beaches in many spots. It seems many men died, but the landings, for now, are a success."

"Good news! I wonder how long it will take them to push inland so we can join them." Gene pondered aloud.

"Not too soon I hope if Francois keeps feeding us like this," Bull joked. We laughed and the news of the invasion taking hold seemed to lighten everyone's mood. I hoped it would be a few days myself. I remembered how it felt when Margaux took my arm and hoped I could feel that again. Ozzy was right and we were cooped up in that cellar for a couple of days. Francois brought bits of news from the front and it soon became apparent we'd have to wait a while to link up with the 101st.

The Germans we engaged were the 17th SS Panzergrenadier Division and headed to give our boys in the 101st one hell of a fight in Carentan. Of course, at the time, we knew none of that. For our part, we dealt them some damage and cost them vital supplies and two pieces of artillery. However, the six of us and some French Resistance fighters weren't going to stop the Nazi counterattack. For the time being, the men of Baker Company were trapped behind enemy lines. But we're Airborne and we had the Krauts right where we wanted them.

EPISODE 2 - ENEMY OF MY ENEMY

It was D-Day plus four. The six men of Baker Company were cooped up in a French Resistance hideout awaiting some word of the invasion and resting up from our raid on the German encampment a few days prior. Well, not all of us were cooped up. Ozzy, who was in charge now after leaving Sarge at a French farmhouse since he was shot on D-Day, had us going on patrols at night. It would have been safer to stay down in the cleverly disguised Maquis hideout but Ozzy wanted us on our toes and he wanted to know what was going on out there.

Cowboy and I were tonight's vict...I mean, volunteers and we'd already stumbled into trouble. We crouched behind a short rock wall not two hundred yards from the entrance to underground hideout as two Krauts approached on a leisurely patrol of their own. They had no reason to be worried since they were a dozen miles from the real action. Even after our attack on the German camp, they had no reason to think there were any Allied forces in their midst this far from the front.

We waited hoping the two soldiers would continue on their way blissfully unaware but instead, they stopped to have a smoke just a few feet from where we hid. They talked quietly as they pulled cigarettes from their uniforms and lit them. Then, one of us made a noise. Not a loud noise, just a shifting of a boot or a buckle scraping on the rock wall. The two soldiers turned our direction and readied their rifles. Fuck!

Cowboy looked at me and almost imperceptibly nodded towards the two. Was he serious? Then his fingers counted down, three, two, one. I guess he was. We both stood suddenly and I pointed my rifle at the soldiers but Cowboy had pulled his Colt revolver, the one he carried back home in Nevada before the war. "Drop 'em, Nazi bastards!" I hissed at the two men who were completely taken by surprise.

One dropped his bolt action and raised his hands immediately. The other held his rifle in shaky hands as he looked from Cowboy to me and back again. He wasn't sure what to do but he was nervous as hell. We had ourselves a little standoff. The soldier who had dropped his rifle said something to his buddy but the man shook his head and muttered something back. I made out "Americanska Devils" or something like that and then the still night was shattered by the unmistakable sound of Cowboy's revolver. The man dropped his rifle, slumped to his knees and then fell over dead. I guess Cowboy heard him call us devils too.

"Fucking Nazis," Cowboy said and then turned his revolver on the other man.

"Don't shoot! I am no Nazi. I am Polish. Please," he pleaded. I glanced at Cowboy but he was still pointing his gun at the soldier.

"What the fuck? Do you think we're stupid?" I asked and shoved my gun at the soldier.

"My name is Lech Ostrowski. I am a Pole. I do not want to die," he told us. Now Cowboy looked at me and I shrugged back.

"If you're Polish, what the fuck are you doing in that Kraut uniform?" I asked. I was curious now but worried this might be a trap. I had to admit, however, that he didn't sound German. I knew some Polish immigrants back in New York and he sounded a lot like them.

"I am a conscript. I was captured by the Soviets in 1939 and held as a prisoner. I was then taken by the Nazis and forced to serve here in defense of France. I am no Nazi. I hate them as much as you," he explained frantically.

"How do you know English?" Cowboy asked the man sounding as curious as he was menacing in his slow western drawl.

"I attended university in America before the war," he answered. I wasn't sure what to think. In any case, we needed to do something. Standing out in the open shooting the shit with a German solider, no matter where he was from, wasn't a good idea.

"What do we do?" I asked Cowboy.

"Fuck, I don't know. We can't just kill him. Take him back with us?" he wondered aloud. He was right. The man had surrendered and now that we knew he might be a prisoner forced to fight, killing him was out of the question.

"This is Fubar. We can't let him go. I guess we have to take him back but Ozzy isn't going to be happy about it," I said. I knew Ozzy would tear us new one for doing it but we didn't have a choice.

"I will go peacefully," Lech told us. I climbed over the wall and searched the dead soldier while Cowboy searched the Polish man. They both carried an ancient bolt action rifle, and not much else besides ammo, which I took from the dead man. Cowboy also found a knife on the polish man, but nothing else of value. A German regular would likely have more than just an old rifle and some ammo on him.

"All right, let's go back and show everyone our new friend," I said to no one in particular. Cowboy followed us keeping an eye on our prisoner and looking out for other soldiers. The Pole didn't give us any trouble and seemed happy to have been captured. He tried to talk to us at one point, but Cowboy told him to shut up. I felt for the guy but I suppose he could have been lying. I guess we'd find out for sure once we got back to the hideout.

These patrols weren't supposed to get us into trouble. They were supposed to be short and sweet just so we knew what was out there and to keep us from getting lazy. Even though Francois brought us news and intelligence, Ozzy wanted his own eyes and ears out here. Gene didn't agree, however. He thought these patrols were pointless and exposed us to unnecessary danger. Maybe he was right. Gene wasn't timid but he was more cautious compared to Ozzy.

Both men were corporals and either could have filled in after Sarge had taken a Kraut bullet to the leg on D-Day but Ozzy was the natural leader. Gene had little desire to lead men but to Ozzy leadership seemed second nature. He was well-liked and sure in his decisions. He could be a hard ass too. Still, Gene wasn't so sure sending us out into the night when there was only six of us was smart. He didn't say it in front of us, but it was apparent the two men had had words about it.

We arrived back at the safe house, an old cellar of a burned out house the French resistance had disguised as a simple pasture with sod planted over the planks of the roof. We found the copse of trees that hid the entrance to the tunnel that led us to the Marquis hideout, found the knotted ropes in the grass and opened the hatch after a last look around. Cowboy and I agreed we should warn everyone before marching our prisoner dressed like a German soldier into the main room. After climbing down the ladder and securing the hatch, Cowboy stayed with Lech as I went through the tunnel to the cellar beyond.

"Where's Cowboy?" Gene asked as I appeared alone. He had a hint of concern in his voice. The rest of our little band, Ozzy, Bull and Jimmy, turned to regard me, each with an uneasy look.

"He's fine. Um...I guess I'll just say it. We have a prisoner," I told them. Gene stood up from the crate he was sitting on. Ozzy set down his poker hand while Jimmy and Bull turned their chairs around as if to watch the show.

"You have a prisoner? A German?" Ozzy asked.

"Yeah...well, no. He's Polish. At least that's what he told us. He says he was captured and forced to serve with the Germans. We relieved him of his weapons and he came willingly. He speaks English," I said. I expected a lecture, but instead Ozzy asked what happened. I gave him the short version.

"So, where is he?" Ozzy asked.

"Cowboy, c'mon," I called and Cowboy led Lech down the tunnel and into the main cellar.

"Holy shit!" Bull exclaimed. Ozzy stood and after a glaring sternly at me and then Cowboy, he walked up to greet the prisoner.

"Polish, huh?" Ozzy asked, looking the man up and down. "How do I know you're not a German pretending to be Polish? How do I know you didn't just tell them that so they wouldn't shoot you too?"

"I am Lech Ostrowski. I come from near Pinsk in eastern Poland. I went to university in America and returned to Poland in 1938 to join the Polish army. In 1939 when the Soviets invaded, I was taken prisoner. I was then liberated by the Nazis only to be pressed into service against the Soviets. Several months ago, I was brought to France to assist in the defense of the Atlantic wall," Lech explained.

"That's all well and good, but anyone could make that up. Why shouldn't I just kill you here and now?" Ozzy asked. I wasn't sure he would really do that but then again, if it meant our survival what else could he do?

"I can give you information. I have no love for the Nazis. I lost family in the invasion of Poland to both the

Nazis and Soviets. I lost many friends that were Jews," Lech explained. Gene came over now to work his way into the conversation.

"What did they do with the Jews?" Gene asked.

"I do not know. I was captured the day after the Soviets invaded. I have heard rumors that many Polish Jews live in large slums and that many have been killed or have died from disease or starvation. I hope that is not true but I fear it is," Lech told us.

"Bastards!" Gene said bitterly. Gene was Jewish and he had joined the paratroopers because he hoped to be the first into Europe. He joined to kill Nazis. He had family in Europe and they had seemingly fallen off the face of the earth. Gene wanted to do what he could to save them or failing that, avenge them.

"I did not want to serve with the Nazis but I had little choice. It was this or a work camp where I would likely die. I am only trying to survive in the hopes I can go home one day and maybe find my family," Lech said. Ozzy looked at Gene, who shrugged as if he didn't have an answer either but both men seemed moved by Lech's answer.

"Lech, you understand we're leery. We need to check this out. We'll hold you until then. If I don't feel like you're legitimate, I'll have to kill you. I have no choice. I can't take prisoners and I can't let you go. If your story checks out, then we can discuss what to do with you. I want to believe you," Ozzy told Lech. The words shook everyone except Lech.

"That is all I can ask," Lech replied and offered his hand. Ozzy took it and they shook hands.

"I'm Corporal Oscar Jennings. Call me Ozzy. Take a seat over there. Cowboy, Tony, you two get to look after our friend until Francois returns. You brought him, you can babysit him," Ozzy announced.

"Ozzy, we didn't have a choice. He surrendered," I explained.

"You're not in trouble, Tony. You did the right thing. Shit happens out there," Ozzy said and slapped me on the back before adding, "But you made the mess so you get to clean it up." Gene started chewing on Ozzy's ear as soon as Cowboy and I took Lech to the far corner.

"That's why we shouldn't be going out on patrols...," Gene started as he followed Ozzy.

"Not in front of the men," Ozzy said and he and Gene disappeared down the tunnel to discuss the issue in private. Ozzy listened to Gene. They were both corporals instead of lowly privates like the rest of us but out here, alone, they might as well have been Eisenhower and Montgomery. Ozzy was firmly in charge, and Gene was OK with that, but when he disagreed with Ozzy he wasn't afraid to say so.

"Have a seat, Lech," I offered. I broke out one of the French cigarettes and offered one to Lech. He took it eagerly.

"Thank you. Are these French?" he asked.

"Yeah. We ran out of Lucky Strikes. You like these?" I replied.

"I am not rationed cigarettes. I only get the German cigarettes I can trade for and I don't have much to trade with. The German officers hoard the French cigarettes," Lech told me.

"They can have them. I'd kill for a pack of Lucky Strikes," I said.

"I preferred Camels when I was in America, but Lucky Strikes are good too," Lech said before bending to let me light his smoke. "If you think the French cigarettes are bad, you should taste the German cigarettes," Lech continued and then wrinkled his nose. That made me laugh.

"Where'd you go to school?" I asked.

"New York. Columbia," Lech said.

"No shit? I'm from Brooklyn," I replied.

"Where did you go to university?" he asked. Now that

was really funny.

"I barely made it out of high school," I told him and Lech laughed. He seemed like a good guy and his story sounded legitimate. I hoped that was the case because Ozzy was right. We couldn't take prisoners.

Cowboy and I took turns watching Lech, who spent most of the night sleeping. I wished I could have done the same. Francois appeared early the next morning. He and Ozzy, as usual, discussed the news of the day. Rumors and reports of the invasion, what the Krauts were up to, etc. After Francois had told Ozzy what he'd heard, Ozzy brought Francois over to see Lech. Francois hadn't seen Lech dressed in a German uniform sitting in the corner with Cowboy and me. When he did, his jaw fell open and he looked at Ozzy with wide eyes.

"Tony and Cowboy found him on patrol last night," Ozzy explained.

"Why did you bring him here?" Francois asked angrily. This was a resistance safe house and now there was a man in a German uniform here. I understood why Francois was upset.

"He surrendered. He says he's Polish. Sounds fishy to me but I wanted to get your take," Ozzy said. Francois looked at Lech and then back to Ozzy.

"Polish, you say? The Nazis have eastern troops. We've come across a few who have deserted, Russians for the most part. He could be telling the truth," Francois said.

"He says he can give us intelligence. Maybe if you can confirm it we can trust him," Ozzy said. Lech watched the exchange nervously. He knew his life depended on what Francois said.

"I cannot think of any other, unless he has papers," Francois said and then turned to Lech, "Do you have identification," in English but slowly.

"I speak English well. Yes, I have papers in my coat," Lech said. I retrieved his coat from a hook on the wall, found the papers and handed them to Francois.

"I can't read these, but I'm looking for Ostlegionen or something similar. That means eastern troops," Francois said. Ozzy and he looked over the papers.

"There," Ozzy said and pointed to the papers.

"Yes, that could be. We would need to ask a German to be sure," Francois replied and then looked to me and asked, "You didn't bring a real German too, did you?" Francois seemed pleased with his little joke. He held out his hand to Lech, "I am Francois. What can you tell me that might help prove to us you are what you say?"

"I am Lech. Happy to meet you, Francois," Lech replied. He detailed troop placements and strengths, mentioned our little adventure of the other night and then mentioned prisoners.

"What kind of prisoners?" Ozzy asked.

"They are British. Paratroopers captured on the day of the invasion and brought to the house that serves as headquarters nearby. Some men in my unit guard them," Lech said.

"We have heard that the Germans may have some prisoners but nothing specific," Francois said.

"What else do you know, Lech?" Ozzy asked. The other men had gathered about after hearing about the prisoners.

"There are three of them. Soldiers like me, mostly Russians though, guard them. The house is lightly defended," Lech told us.

"I will see what I can discover. If his story checks out, what are we going to do?" Francois asked.

"If his story checks out we'll go get those men," Ozzy said plainly without a moment's hesitation.

"What? I meant what are we going to do about the Pole. I am not sure rescuing the English prisoner is prudent," Francois said.

"We can't leave them there. Our job isn't to be prudent. If it was, we wouldn't be in this mess. We'd be back home reading about the war," Ozzy said. Francois nodded.

"I forget. You are soldiers. The Maquis are not. We all may die in battle but you will likely not be lined up against a wall and shot if you are captured," Francois said.

"I suppose not. You don't have to go," Ozzy said.

"You know I will go. Henry too. Margaux will insist on coming with us also," Francois said. I perked up at that. I didn't want her to go with us. I hadn't seen her since the night we got back from destroying the German guns, but I remembered it fondly. I could still almost feel her warm body pressed next to mine. I held my tongue though.

"Thank you, friend. We appreciate everything you've done for us," Ozzy said.

"No, we appreciate what you are doing. At times, I am ashamed American and British soldiers must die to liberate France. You will give us our country back," Francois replied.

"So we're going after the Brits?" Gene asked. I thought he might be ready to argue against it as he had against the evening patrols. We didn't have to do it and it exposed us to unnecessary risk. He didn't though.

"Yeah, I can't leave them there in good conscience if we can get them out," Ozzy said obviously thinking Gene might disagree.

"I agree. I'm looking forward to the opportunity," Gene said. Ozzy nodded.

"I don't know when we leave, but we all need to get ready. It might be as soon as tonight. Clean your weapons, gather and redistribute the ammo, you know the drill," Ozzy ordered.

"Might I be allowed to accompany you?" Lech asked.

"I don't think so," Ozzy said and then approached Lech, "You want to help? Tell us everything you know, draw us a map, give us sentry schedules, whatever you got. If it's accurate and helps us out, we'll talk," Ozzy said.

"I will tell you anything you want," Lech responded.

Gene looked at him and then to Ozzy.

"Didn't he say his unit was guarding the prisoners?" Gene asked. Ozzy seemed to understand where Gene was headed with that.

"What about that? Why would you give us information that might harm other soldiers like you?" Ozzy asked.

"They are mostly Soviet. I like them even less than the Nazis," Lech said with obvious disgust. Everyone had heard about the Nazi invasion of Poland in '39, but the Russians invaded Poland too. All that was before Hitler turned on Stalin and attacked Russia opening up the eastern front. The Krauts and the Russians held what was left of Poland. Something told me the Russians didn't treat the Polish much better than the Germans had and from the stuff I'd heard that wasn't saying much.

"Fair enough. Still, I can't risk it," Ozzy said and Gene seemed to agree. I liked Lech, but even I was skeptical. His uniform wasn't helping matters. It just reminded me that he might be lying to us. I didn't think he was but how could anyone be sure? I'd lie to save my skin and protect my buddies if I was captured. For all we knew, we were walking into a trap.

We spent the rest of the morning sorting ammo, cleaning weapons and getting everything together. Ozzy and Gene spent the time grilling Lech. He showed them the location of the house on the map and even drew a crude interior layout. He gave us specific information about number of guards, troop sizes and locations and what kind of weapons they had. It seemed the Germans weren't too worried about an attack this far behind the lines and the house was lightly defended. If we were quick, we might be able to get in an out without much trouble, but things never seemed to work out the way we hoped.

Lech also told us what he had heard about our attack on the German camp the other night. Seems those weren't just any Krauts. They were SS troops, advance elements of the 17th SS Panzergrenadiers headed to engage the 101st

Airborne at Carentan. That's where we were supposed to be. It appeared the Germans thought the attack was launched by scouts from the paratrooper units in front of them along with resistance fighters, not a ragtag band of paratroopers lost somewhere behind them in Normandy. In any case, they had a couple of dozen fewer men and two fewer eighty-eights to fight with.

Francois returned that evening. Margaux was with him as was Henry. He confirmed what Lech had told us about the British paratroopers and which house they were being held. It was, indeed, lightly defended. Francois told us he and Henry would be coming with us. They had been to the house that morning, or at least close enough to scout it out, and could help us find it in the dark. The French had an advantage there. They could wander around openly during the day. It was their country, after all. As long as they were subtle, they could gather all sorts of intelligence. With Lech's information, we gathered around and formulated a plan.

It was decided that Francois and Henry would provide cover and serve as lookouts. They were brave but not experienced and didn't have the training we had. Each would take up positions near the house, keep an eye out for trouble and determine our best route of escape based on conditions. The rest of us would enter the house and rescue the Brits.

Ozzy and Jimmy would find the Brits, Bull and I would load up on weapons and ammo and Gene and Cowboy would watch our backs. We had enough ammo for this operation and maybe for a while afterwards but we had no idea how long we might be isolated. Ozzy, after seeing what we had left, decided we needed to get some German guns, ammo and grenades. The Maquis had some weapons but we needed more. At some point, it was possible we would run out of ammo and then we could only hope the Allies made it inland sooner rather than later.

According to Lech, the house had a cache of small

arms, ammo and grenades, more than enough to last us for months, but we could only carry so much. We all emptied our packs and Bull and I would fill them and redistribute them before we left. The Germans used mostly bolt-action rifles, that were generally inferior to our M1 rifles and carbines, and machine pistols that were at least the equal of our Thompsons. The Germans used the potato masher grenades for the most part and they had their advantages, but our smaller pineapple and baseball grenades were a lot easier to carry.

Now, all I had to do was try to convince Margaux not to go if she intended to. After we finalized our plans, we all filled our bellies and then settled in to wait until nightfall. I'd hoped Margaux would join me, but she didn't. She kept to herself instead. Finally, I wandered over to her. She looked up as I sat next to her.

"Hello, Tony," she greeted me.

"Hey, you seem upset," I told her.

"I am," was all she said.

"Are you going tonight? On the mission with us, I mean," I asked, expecting her to say she was and then I wondered if I should try to talk her out of it. Even after she and Francois saved our asses a few nights back, I had a hard time with the idea this pretty French girl was a freedom fighter. I didn't want to think of her that way and I didn't want her to get hurt.

"Did my father say something?" she asked. I shook my head. "He will not allow me to go. I will stay here and guard the Polish soldier," she indicated. I was relieved but leaving her alone with the big Pole didn't seem prudent either. My gut told me Lech was telling us the truth but if he wasn't he could easily overpower Margaux.

"Alone?" I asked.

"No, a few men will join me soon. It is an excuse so my father can keep me from going with you," she spat with thinly veiled contempt. She was a brave woman and I admired her spirit but I couldn't help wanting to protect her. I understood exactly where Francois was coming from.

"I'm glad you'll be here instead of out there," I said not realizing what that implied.

"So, just because I am a woman I cannot fight? I have just as much reason as anyone. My mother was raped and killed by the Nazis but I am to stay here and tend to a prisoner?" Margaux challenged, her voice growing louder. A few of the others must have heard and looked over at us.

"I didn't know that. I'm sorry. I think your father just wants to protect his daughter," I said and Margaux's stern expression softened.

"Maybe. Why do you not want me to go?" she asked.

"I don't want to see you get hurt either," I said honestly. Margaux smiled and looked away, but her hand found mine. For a moment, she didn't speak. She looked up at me still smiling.

"Thank you. Oh, I almost forgot. I brought you something," she said, taking me by surprise. What would she have brought me? Margaux reached into her coat and pulled out an entire carton of Lucky Strikes.

"Where the fuck...I mean, where did you get those?" I asked. Margaux laughed softly.

"I know people," she said cryptically. I ripped into the package and pulled out a pack, put it to my nose and inhaled deeply. Suddenly Jimmy and Ozzy were there with us.

"Where did those come from? You been holding out on us, Tony?" Jimmy asked.

"Margaux brought them. Can I?" I asked Margaux. I wanted to make sure she didn't mind if I shared. She smiled and nodded.

"They are yours," Margaux told me.

"Thanks! This is great. Here you go, you bums. Lech, you get a pack too," I said handing two packs each to Jimmy and Ozzy and tossing one over to Lech. Bull and

Cowboy chewed tobacco and it seemed they both had plenty stashed in their gear. Made sense because chewing tobacco wasn't part of our rations. Gene didn't smoke. I kept the rest, hoping to trade them for something later. Or maybe I'd just smoke them all myself.

I lit up a pair of the Lucky Strikes and handed one to Margaux. Damn, that tasted good and suddenly everything seemed just a little bit better. I sat with Margaux until it was time to get ready. Two men showed and Francois directed them to watch Lech but not to hurt him. Francois explained he was Polish, not German. That's what Margaux told me he said anyway. The men apparently didn't speak English.

We each had a good supply of ammo still and we'd divided the remaining clips and grenades equally. I had about a hundred and twenty rounds for my M1 and half a dozen grenades, though half of those stayed behind. The other guys had about the same. Ozzy reminded us to conserve ammo but only if it made sense. No sense saving ammo if you weren't around to use it later. Francois and Henry had secured German rifles and some ammo captured by the Maquis. It was almost twenty-two hundred hours when we left the security of the safe house.

Margaux saw us off, hugging her father and Henry, kissing each of us on the cheeks except for me. I got a hug along with my kiss. Cowboy turned and smiled knowingly at me and I punched him in the arm. He chuckled and Bull joined in. As we walked down the tunnel Ozzy said, "Hey, leave lover boy alone you two." Now everyone laughed and even I joined in. The mood didn't last, however. As soon as we emerged into the cool night air, we all got a lot more serious.

Francois and Henry scouted ahead and after a moment, they declared the area clear. We followed, Cowboy taking point and Ozzy taking up the rear. Francois walked behind Cowboy and directed him where to go. As we had during our raid on the Kraut camp, we used cover as much as possible. Occasionally, we were forced to cross a road or an open field, but for the most part we stuck to the hedgerows or stayed among the trees.

We spotted a German patrol after we'd traveled about a mile, but they were a hundred and fifty yards off. We got low and quiet and they passed us by without incident. Francois had told us the Germans were on alert after the attack on the encampment a few nights ago, but not actively searching for anyone. That was D-Day plus one and now it was D-Day plus five. The Krauts still assumed they were attacked by scouts or advance elements of the allied invasion. I guess in a way, we were advance elements, though entirely unintentional advanced elements. In any case, they weren't looking for Americans in their midst and they were relatively relaxed.

We were going to change that.

Another hour of sneaking through dense trees and along thick hedgerows and Francois called the party to a halt. We moved through the trees quietly and once we reached the other side of the small grove, we saw the house. It was a couple of hundred yards away. There was plenty of cover for us to use, fences, walls, trees and brush. A road ran past the front of the house and guards manned the drive. We were going to bypass them, however.

So far, Lech's intelligence was dead on, the road, the drive leading up to the house, the guards and the lack of any lights. Lights weren't a good idea in Nazi-occupied France. Allied planes used them for targets. However, barely visible slits of light leaked here and there from the drapes. We had all committed the interior layout of the house to memory. Ozzy pulled us back from the edge of the trees so we could discuss what we had seen.

"If the Pole is right, the Brits are upstairs in that room with the window boarded. Did you see it, Jimmy?"

"Yeah, Ozzy," Jimmy answered. Jimmy wasn't as skittish as he'd been on our previous outing. We were all scared, but he seemed to have it under control. I was sure he'd be the first man to break but Jimmy did all right. We all did, honestly. Considering the circumstances, it was a wonder we all weren't losing our heads.

"The weapons are in a storage room near the rear entrance. We'll go in that way. The stairs are at the center of the house, more or less. Gene, Cowboy, you hold that door no matter what. Francois, either you or Henry stays here. The other should move to the far side of the house. Like we agreed, if you see anything that might jeopardize our escape or trap us in that house, start shooting. That'll be the signal to get the hell out of Dodge," Ozzy said going over the plan one last time.

Francois nodded and said, "I will leave Henry here and I'll take up position down the road." He then turned and translated all that for Henry.

"Remember, we're playing this one by ear. We don't know how many Krauts are in that house or where the sentries are. Stay alert. Remember your training. Stay safe. If you get separated, hunker down and wait for things to shake out, then navigate back to the safe house and don't get followed. You stay safe too, Francois," Ozzy said. He shook Francois' hand and then Henry's. Francois moved off towards his position and then the six of us moved off in the opposite direction.

We followed the tree line and after a couple hundred yards, we pushed through the trees and finding no sentries, we crossed the road, two by two. We made it across the road without incident and then we made our way through the sparse forest that surrounded the house. We called it a house, but back home it would be called a mansion. Here, I think the French referred to places like this as manors. The place was as big as the building I lived in as a kid, but we shared that with three other families.

We reached the brick wall surrounding the manor and moved along the wall towards the back of the house. The wall was more for privacy than security. We found a latticed wooden gate set in an arched opening in the wall.

From that vantage we could see two sentries walking amongst the manicured courtyard within and a guard at the rear door on the broad landing that served as a porch. None of them looked to be alerted to our presence or especially concerned. The guard at the back door smoked as he leaned against the rear of the house. The sentries walked lazily and without purpose.

The courtyard was a maze of hedges, walls, benches, flower beds and small trees. In other words, there was plenty of cover, especially without any artificial light. The trees filtered the moonlight and shaded the gardens for the most part. Once Ozzy had the lay of the land, he turned to us and signaled how he wanted this to go down. Rifles weren't an option. Even a single shot would alert every Kraut for miles. These three guards would have to be taken out hand to hand.

Ozzy and Jimmy would stay back as the rest of us would dispatch the Germans. Jimmy's leg was still torn up and he was taking it easy as best he could. One guard was working his way towards us and we'd wait until we could surprise him. Bull would take him. I'd provide cover in case things got out of hand, but Ozzy was clear that I wasn't to shoot unless I had no other choice. Gene would take the other guard wandering the courtyard as Cowboy went for the guard at the back door. If he could chase down a wayward calf, he could close the ground and silence that guard.

The first guard wandered near and then turned to wander back the other direction. I opened the gate slowly and Bull got ready to rush the guard with Gene and Cowboy right behind him. Bull was about to go when the gate creaked and the guard turned. It was a small noise but enough to grab his attention. As he turned, Bull was already on him and then guard's eyes went wide as Bulls big hand covered him mouth and his knife sank into the German's neck.

Bull laid the dead man down and turned to join me as

we took up positions to cover Gene and Cowboy. They rushed past the guard Bull has just killed. Gene picked his way amongst the cover as he approached the wandering guard. Cowboy, on the other hand, took a more direct route. The man at the backdoor never saw the shadowy figure that charged until it was too late, but he did manage to utter something before Cowboy tackled him and they both flew over the far side of the landing at the top of the back steps.

The man Gene stalked turned at the commotion and saw Gene immediately. I saw the guard draw his knife as Gene tackled the man. I didn't waste a moment. I took off towards the melee. I expected to find two men in a battle for their lives but instead, I found Gene straddling the dead Kraut. The German's eyes were wide and glazed, a knife protruded from his chest and blood ran from his mouth.

"Burn in hell, fucker," Gene whispered as he yanked the knife from the man's chest. He got to his feet and noticed I was standing behind him.

"I thought he was going to get the best of you," I explained quietly.

"I've been waiting years to look into one of these bastard's eyes as he died," was all Gene said as he brushed past me to find the others. I followed to find Ozzy and Jimmy waiting near the gate and we all made our way to the house where Cowboy and Bull waited. The man Cowboy had taken down was lying on the ground near the steps and I could see the dark pool of blood fed by a gaping wound in his neck. I didn't have time to reflect, however. Gene and Cowboy would wait here and cover our escape while the rest of us lined up ready to infiltrate the house.

Bull and I stood in front of the door as Ozzy slowly opened it. My heart was pounding but everything paused as we heard artillery in the distance. The first evidence of the invasion we'd heard since we hit the ground. We listened to it for a moment and the sound seemed to fill us all with a little hope. That's how I felt anyway. Ozzy opened the door further and there was nothing there. Just a small room with a hallway beyond illuminated by a dim light from the main part of the house.

Bull and I went in and took up positions on either side of the door leading to the hallway. Ozzy and Jimmy were right behind us and they entered the hallway carefully. Then we heard it. Someone speaking in German. We paused but it was clear immediately that it was a radio. Whether anyone listened, no one knew. Ozzy and Jimmy proceeded and as they did, pointed to a doorway along the way. The weapons room, I assumed.

I nodded and then looked towards the back door but Cowboy and Gene weren't anywhere to be seen. They had likely found cover. I turned to Bull and he nodded at me. We abandoned the small room and followed Ozzy and Jimmy down the hall and then ducked into the doorway they had indicated. Bull and I quickly pulled off our packs and began stuffing them with anything we could find. We left the bolt actions behind and opted for the MP40s, the German's effective and deadly machine pistols. Those went into my pack as Bull filled his with ammo and then we both stuffed German potato mashers amongst the rest.

"Tony!" Bull whispered. It was dark but our eyes were adjusted and the faint glow from down the hall provided enough light so we could see. He threw his back against the wall and I knew he had heard something. I knelt and sank into the shadows as a single pair of boots approached. A German wandered by peeking into the room we occupied but he had come from the front of the house and his eyes saw nothing but darkness apparently.

He muttered something in German and his step quickened. The back door was open! I stood and peered into the hall but the soldier was gone. Then Gene peered inside and I caught his eye. He gave me the thumbs up and disappeared again. I ducked back inside the weapons room as Bull looked at me expectantly.

"They got him," I whispered. Bull shrugged and we went back to work.

"Holy shit," Bull whispered after a few seconds. He bent and came back up with a long cylindrical object. "A fucking Panzerschreck," he said quietly. Indeed, Bull held a long tube that looked a lot like our bazookas but with a shield attached to the middle.

"That might come in handy. Where's the ammo?" I asked, but I was already searching.

"Here's a whole bunch," Bull said and handed me the big cannon. He lifted several large wooden crates and set them on the boxes of rifle ammo.

"You can't carry those?" I said. Together the four boxes must have weighed a hundred pounds.

"The hell I can't," he said. Just then we heard movement and then a cry came from the front of the house. It was German. Then a single gunshot rang out and many boots came down the hallway.

"We've got to go!" Ozzy said harshly as he passed the weapons room. Bull and I shouldered our packs. Mine must've weighed as much as those boxes of Panzerschreck ammo. Men rushed by the door, first Jimmy, then three other men, the Brits I assumed.

"Help me!" Bull said and I turned to see him struggling with ammo crates. I helped him lift them as he ducked and we managed to get the boxes on his shoulders. He was barely able to stand up, but he managed and I went out the door. I covered our escape as Bull followed the rest of our squad. A Kraut appeared at the end of the hall and I shouldered my rifle and took him out. Two more appeared and returned fire. Bullets whizzed by as I fired back.

"Go Bull!" I shouted, but he was already in the room beyond. I backed away and finally turned and ran, or rather lumbered with the pack full of weapons and ammo on my back. Bullets hit the door frame as I dashed through and I heard a hollow clang as a bullet hit something metal. I went right past the group huddled in the room near the back door and out into the courtyard. Cowboy caught me as I stumbled down the stairs and the rest were piling out the back door behind me.

It reminded me of jumping out of the C-47 transport as men poured through the door. The second to last man out, a Brit, gasped and went down clutching at his back. He was dead when he hit the stairs. Ozzy was the last out and he closed the door behind himself. Gene was leading Bull, Jimmy and the two remaining British paratroopers towards the gate. Ozzy and Cowboy took up positions around the door.

"Go, Tony," Ozzy shouted. I turned and followed the rest of the group to the gate. We hunkered down on the far side of the wall. Now lights were on everywhere and there were Germans shouting and giving orders. So much for a quiet getaway. Then the back door burst open. Several Krauts emerged but Ozzy and Cowboy let them pass. When four German soldiers stood on the landing surveying the courtyard, Ozzy peeled away from the side of the steps and let them have it with his Tommy gun.

Cowboy hopped onto the landing and emptied his clip through the open door as he crouched amongst the dead Germans. I could hear screams and shouts inside. Cowboy and Ozzy ran for their lives towards the gate and never stopped. We all followed them along the wall and then through the hedges and trees back the way we'd come. All hell was breaking loose and Krauts were everywhere. Still, it seemed we might have pulled this off if only we could get across the road and into the cover beyond. We reached the road crossing and Ozzy sent Jimmy and the Brits across first while we watched. They made it but then we heard a Kraut yelling.

We all turned and a single soldier called out and more appeared. He'd seen the three men crossing the road. More Germans joined him but they didn't advance or fire on us. They waited instead. On the opposite side of the road, Henry met the Brits and led them into the cover beyond. We, on the other hand, were trapped. I hoped the German's didn't know we were there and that's why they hesitated. Then we heard a rumbling and the Krauts retreated.

"Half-track!" Gene whispered. Sure enough, from behind the house a German half-track appeared with at least twenty men following using it for cover.

"Shit!" Ozzy swore, but then he looked at me. "You got ammo for that thing?" Ozzy inquired and Bull pat the boxes he still carried on his shoulder. "Well, don't just sit there," Ozzy told him. We were in heavy cover near the road as the half-track approached but if they saw us, they'd cut us to pieces with the machine gun mounted to the top of that thing. The Krauts fanned out now, searching the area as the half-track shined its spotlight all about.

Bull was fumbling with a box of ammo and Gene was trying to help. "Hurry the fuck up," Ozzy demanded.

"We're working on it," Gene replied angrily.

"Look!" I said. Ozzy followed my gaze and we could both clearly see Francois about a hundred yards down the road on the opposite side, halfway up a tree.

"Well, I'll be," Ozzy said. Now, everyone looked as the half-track approached his hiding spot. Then the light from the metal beast hit us square and men shouted as they saw us. "Get down!" Ozzy shouted. Gene and Bull were still working on the crate of ammo as the machine gunner opened up on our position. They abandoned the ammo box as we all hit the ground to avoid the deadly fire. The trees and branches above us were cut to pieces. We had only the cover provided by the road embankment but that was barely enough to protect us. Dirt, leaves and splintered wood showered us as the withering machine gun fire had us pinned down.

Krauts were shouting and yelling as the half-track approached, spitting lead at us. It wouldn't be long before even the meager cover the road embankment provided wouldn't be enough. Then the night lit up like daytime and the ground shook with a deafening explosion. Men screamed and ran as the half-track rolled to a stop, burning and ruined. Francois! I looked but he was gone from his perch. I wasn't sure what he had done but I knew Francois had done it.

"Get your shit and let's get the fuck out of here," Ozzy roared. We all got up and we all helped carry the Panzerschreck ammo this time. Ozzy and Cowboy traded fire with the Germans who weren't lying dead on the road behind the ruined half-track. Then two men appeared across the road.

"Yanks! Let's go!" the older of the two shouted. Bull and I were the first to venture out into the open. The burning half-track provided a nice bit of cover now. Bullets rang off its metal body as we dove into the trees amongst the Brits. "Good show!" the older man said in a proper English accent and pat me on the shoulder. Ozzy, Cowboy and Gene were still on the wrong side of the road, however.

"There are guns in my pack," I told the two men and they dug in. Both came out with MP40s and then they found magazines, loaded and ready to go in amongst the tangle of at least a half dozen other machine pistols.

"Outstanding! Let's get a little payback for ol' Neville," the older man said.

"Aye, Lieutenant," the young, stockier man said in a distinct Scottish brogue. The two men slapped magazines into their machine pistols, yanked back the bolt and let it go. They tore into the Germans, though they likely didn't hit any of them. It was cover fire and the three men across the road took advantage. They ran crouched, carrying a couple of the ammo crates, and dove amongst us. The Germans were scattered but regrouping now and beginning to advance. We shrank further into the trees.

"What now, Corporal?" the British Lieutenant asked deferring to Ozzy. Henry appeared a moment later.

Francois was nowhere to be seen.

"Uh...the...way...," Henry struggled to explain but the Lieutenant broke in.

"En Francais," he told Henry and he answered the British Lieutenant in French.

"He says the way is clear. He's scouted ahead and he found no enemy," the Lieutenant translated.

"Gene, take Tony's pack. Jimmy, grab that shoulder cannon. You two," Ozzy said to the Brits, "grab a couple of these ammo boxes. Tony, you take point, I've got the rear," Ozzy said and we all moved. Moments later, we were moving further into the trees leaving the Germans behind. Or so we thought. It wasn't long as we moved amongst the trees and hedgerows before we heard German's all around us and saw lights moving about.

Now I heard distinct Russian voices among the Germans. We were moving slow with all the ammo. None of us were injured but it didn't matter. We needed to get out of the area before we were surrounded. If we were, we'd have to wait this out and hope we weren't found. An armored car and motorcycles moved up and down the road we'd crossed looking for us. There were Germans coming out of the woodwork like termites.

"Ozzy, we need to leave this stuff," Gene said.

"I'm afraid you're right. Damn," Ozzy replied and we huddled into a copse of trees. We still hadn't seen a German patrol directly, but it was probably just a matter of time.

"Corporal, we can do a lot of good with these arms. How much further?" the Lieutenant asked.

"At least a half mile, a kilometer," Ozzy said but Henry held up two fingers. "Looks like closer to two," he corrected. The British Lieutenant shook his head. We all knew what he was thinking. We were thinking it too. We were likely going to be captured or die fighting. Just then, a half dozen Krauts happened upon us. We never saw them but when one shouted and they turned their flashlights on us, it was too late.

The Scotsman fired first and Cowboy and I were right behind him. The Lieutenant took a bullet and went down. Ozzy, yanked a grenade from his suspenders and threw it into the German's midst. We turned as the pineapple went off and killed or wounded the entire squad. But our position was compromised and others were headed our way. The Scot looked after his Lieutenant who had been hit in the shoulder. I caught Ozzy's eye and he looked resigned to our fate. He dropped the magazine out of his Thompson and slammed a fresh one home.

We'd done our best but there were too many Krauts and we had too far to travel. The Lieutenant was up again, a makeshift bandage around his shoulder and he checked his machine pistol. We all followed suit, readying grenades and checking magazines. No words were necessary. We knew we had to fight our way out of this and that we would likely die here amongst the hedgerows somewhere in Normandy. At least we'd take a few of the Kraut bastards with us.

A small patrol appeared but they were ready for us. The exchange of fire and the grenade explosion had given us away. They dropped to the ground as they saw us and began firing and shouting to the other Krauts in the area. "Remember, every Nazi we kill here is one our boys on the beaches won't have to kill later," Ozzy reminded us. We all knew this wasn't going to turn out well.

"It's been an honor, Yanks," the Lieutenant said with a finality that was unmistakable. The Germans were joined by others and soon more appeared behind us and took up positions to prevent our escape. I looked around at the men of Baker Company, the Brits and the lone Frenchman. Nobody would ever know what we did here. If we were lucky, some Allied soldiers would happen upon our bodies and collect our dog tags so our families would know what happened to us. I thought of my mom and pop. I felt bad that they were about to lose their boy.

The Germans didn't fire, not yet. They had us and now at least thirty Krauts had surrounded us. Maybe they'd ask us to surrender. I don't think anyone in our small band was willing to give up, however. For a moment, it was almost peaceful. Germans were moving at the edge of our sight, digging in and readying for a fight. They probably had no idea how many men they faced and they weren't taking any chances. It was only a matter of time, however.

Then behind us, the sky lit up as an explosion rocked the area. We all turned and saw a cloud of fire and smoke rise into the air over the trees behind us and fade into the night. Then another explosion, less intense this time, followed. The Germans around us began shouting and many of them rushed towards the chaos. Suddenly, we weren't the main focus any longer.

"Take 'em!" Ozzy shouted and we all opened up. Maybe ten Krauts remained behind and we traded fire with them as others fled to defend their headquarters. Suddenly, we had a fighting chance. I had no idea what had caused that explosion but it might just have saved our asses. I didn't have much time to think about it as bullets whizzed past us and hit the trees we hid amongst with deadly thumps.

"Do you think you can get one of those crates open and figure out how that cannon works?" Ozzy asked Bull and Gene after their previous failure.

"I've got it, laddies," the Scotsman said and pulled his revolver from its holster, though Cowboy's was much larger. He didn't fiddle with the fasteners, instead just shooting them off but carefully so as to avoid the rockets inside. Bull had the Panzerschreck ready as he knelt behind a tree. The Scot threw open the box and then handed a rocket to his compatriot. The Lieutenant passed it to Gene, who then loaded the big cannon.

"Is this all I do?" Gene asked. Cowboy, Ozzy and I were firing on the Germans, pinning them down and giving Bull and Gene a chance to fire the weapon. Henry

Dan McMartin

tried to keep up with his bolt action, but it was no match for our M1s and Tommy guns. Suddenly, Gene cried out and went down. The Lieutenant took his place instantly.

"Lieutenant, plug in those wires," the Scot told him. The elder Brit found them and after examining the weapon, connected them to the tube. "Now, out of the way!" the Scot shouted. Bull leaned around the tree that barely managed to hide his broad form, seconds passed as he lined up a shot.

"Shoot the fucking thing," Ozzy yelled as he changed magazines again.

"I've never fired a Kraut bazooka. Give me a second," Bull replied. A bullet hit just short of Cowboy and he got a face full of dirt and grass. Then, as my magazine popped free and ran out as all M1s did, Bull launched the rocket. It left us in a cloud of acrid, billowing smoke and soared towards the Germans. It appeared to have hit short, but it didn't matter. The action stopped on both sides. We waited anxiously to see if the Krauts were done for. Then we heard a painful cry from their position.

"Cowboy, Tony, go clean that up," Ozzy yelled. "I'll cover them, the rest of you gather everything and get going," Ozzy ordered but he wasn't aware that Gene had been hit.

"Ozzy, Gene's down," Bull told him. Cowboy and I headed towards the Kraut position, crouching low as we left Gene to the rest of the group. Nothing moved ahead but we could hear at least one man moaning. He wasn't moving when we found him. The rocket hit the Krauts dead on and tore them apart. I almost felt sorry for the poor bastards, almost. We made our way back to the group. Gene was up and alert when we returned. He'd taken a round off his helmet. It had a serious dent where the bullet had ricocheted off the steel pot. He was up but woozy. We moved out carrying all the weapons and ammo we'd managed to pilfer.

Cowboy and I followed Henry and Ozzy and the Scot

60

took up the rear. We all shared the crates of Panzerschreck ammo and even Jimmy with his bum leg had a pack full of ammo and grenades. We moved as fast as we could. Cover wasn't as much of a consideration now. Getting to safety was our main goal. The pursuit had ceased and the sky behind us was bright with the fire that burned where the manor we'd attacked stood. I half expected we'd meet up with a column of Sherman tanks but it never happened.

"What the hell, happened back there?" Jimmy asked finally.

"I have no idea," Cowboy replied.

"Whatever it was, it saved our asses," Bull said.

"Shut up, girls!" Ozzy scolded us. We remained quiet the rest of the way. It took us almost an hour to get back to the safe house. Even then, Henry insisted on going back and making sure we weren't followed before we went to the copse of trees that hid the entrance to the old basement.

"I thought you said there was a house about, Yank," the Lieutenant mentioned as we waited for Henry to return.

"It's right over there," Ozzy said grinning. The Lieutenant looked where Ozzy pointed and then looked back at the Scotsman puzzled. Henry came back and said something to the Brit who translated.

"He says we weren't followed," the Lieutenant indicated and we headed for the entrance. We went in, two by two keeping an eye out for Kraut patrols. Once everyone else was inside, Bull and the Scotsman lowered the heavy packs and the boxes of rockets down to Ozzy, Cowboy and me. Henry kept watch as they entered the tunnel and then followed himself once he was satisfied no one had seen us.

Margaux greeted us looking for her father as she did. It dawned on me suddenly that Francois wasn't with us. I didn't know where he was. No one had seen him since I spotted him in the tree near the half-track. I set down my gear and found Margaux looking confused and hurt.

"We got separated. He was alive when we saw him last," I assured her and then it all came into focus. He had destroyed the half-track and I was sure he had caused the explosions that saved all of us. "He saved us all. I'm sure he'll be back soon," I told Margaux but she didn't look convinced. I took her aside and sat with her. I hoped I was right. Gene was still woozy and the British Lieutenant's bandage was soaked with blood but the bullet had passed through his shoulder and the wound was clean.

"I think Francois blew up the half-track and maybe the house too," I announced, pleased with my detective work. Ozzy looked at me and rolled his eyes.

"You think?" he said and laughed. I guess it wasn't that much a stretch.

"I didn't even think of that," Jimmy replied.

"That's why I'm in charge," Ozzy joked. Jimmy frowned, but couldn't help but laugh. We all laughed, even Margaux though her father was missing. It felt good to be able to laugh. It felt good to be alive. We all quieted down as the early morning wore on. I don't know about the other guys, but the whole thing kind of hit me and I realized how close we were to dying. I pulled out my Lucky Strikes and offered one to Margaux and then took my own. The Zippo was shaking as I lit our smokes or maybe it was me.

I held Margaux as Gene patched up the Brit and everyone else sorted through the gear. I think they all understood why I was sitting with Margaux. Henry came over to us at one point and said something to her. I think it was about Francois. Margaux smiled and took his hand.

"Merci, Henry," she told the Frenchman. Henry disappeared up the tunnel and I heard the hatch open and close. "He is going to search for my father," she said.

"I'll go with him," I said. Ozzy turned but Margaux beat him to the punch.

"Dressed like that?" she asked pointedly. I guess she

was right. An American soldier probably shouldn't be out wandering about after what we'd done tonight.

"You're right," I said. I caught Ozzy looking my way. He shook his head and rolled his eyes. Gene finished patching up the British Lieutenant. He and his fellow paratrooper approached Ozzy.

"We've not been properly introduced. I'm Lieutenant James Graham. This is Sergeant Embry Stewart," Lieutenant Graham announced.

"Corporal Oscar Jennings," Ozzy said and then introduced each of us in turn by our rank and full name but added our nicknames too. "You can call me Ozzy. We're pretty informal around here. I guess you're in command now, Lieutenant," Ozzy said. That grabbed everyone's attention. Technically, Lieutenant did outrank Corporal. In fact, Sergeant did too. The British soldiers looked confused, however.

"Call me James then and we call Sergeant Stewart, Ember. So am I to take it that you're in command? Where are you officers? You have other men, surely," James asked.

"Uh...I hate to tell you this, but you're looking at it," Ozzy said and then explained. He told the Brits about the C-47 and how only seven of us made it out. He told the Brits about our Sarge and his injury, the attack on the Germans, Lech, who looked on with much interest, and about our plan to rescue them. "Sorry about your man," Ozzy offered, referring to the British soldier killed back at the manor, when he was done with his tale.

"Ah, yes. Thank you. Neville was a good man. We appreciate your daring. I doubt Fritz would have harmed us, but we'd rather not have to spend the war in a prison camp," James replied.

"Yes, thank you," Ember added.

"Happy to do it," Ozzy told them.

"I must ask, Ozzy, who's the Jerry in the corner?" James asked. We called the Germans Krauts but the Brits referred to them as Jerry or Fritz.

"Oh, he's Polish. He was captured in Poland when the Soviets invaded and then pressed into service by the Krauts. He gave us the information we needed to free you," Ozzy said and went to Lech and shook his hand. "I trust you, we trust you. James, you owe this man a debt of gratitude. He's called Lech... Ostrowski?" Ozzy introduced him, though he struggled with the last name.

"Yes, thank you," Lech said. Ozzy looked at him and then grabbed the swastika on his uniform and yanked it free.

"We'll have to find you some better clothes," Ozzy said. Lech nodded.

"Thank you, Lech. If these men trust you, then so shall we," James said and went to shake the Pole's hand. I watched this as I sat with Margaux. Just then, Henry appeared in the tunnel. Margaux stood and Henry stepped aside as Francois appeared out of the darkened tunnel.

"Papa!" Margaux exclaimed and ran to her father. Francois hugged his daughter and lifted her from the ground. I was almost as glad to see him as she was. After hearing about her mother and what the Nazis did to her, I didn't want anything to happen to Francois.

"How did you like my little Independence Day celebration?" Francois asked once he let his daughter go.

"You're a month early," Ozzy told the Frenchman.

"Maybe it was for French independence," Francois joked and went to Ozzy and the men hugged. Ozzy introduced the Brits to the Frenchman, who thanked him for helping their release.

"How did you pull that off?" Gene asked.

"What kind of resistance fighter would I be if I didn't carry explosives?" Francois answered. Gene laughed.

"Well, you saved our asses twice. Thank you, friend," Ozzy told the Frenchman. Dawn was coming and we were all hungry and tired. Francois asked the men who had been guarding Lech to patrol the area before heading to their homes. Once the sun was up no one could leave or enter. Not with the Krauts on alert and they were sure to be on alert.

We cleaned up and stowed our gear. Taking inventory of the Kraut weapons could wait. Margaux broke out more than enough wine, cheese, bread and cured meat for everyone. We all took our fill, we'd earned it. I finished my meal with a Lucky Strike along with Margaux. The carton was going fast but I let each of the Brits have a pack too.

"Thank you, Tony is it?" James replied.

"No problem. Thank the lady. She found them somewhere," I said. The Brits did thank her and then I went to find a quiet corner to catch a nap. Margaux joined me and sat between my legs. "I'm dirty," I told her.

"Should I leave then?" she asked.

"No, no. Stay," I said and she smiled. The whole night was a blur now. Bits and pieces were clear as day but others were just a jumble in my head. I wasn't shaking anymore though. Gene was out, still a little punchy from getting his bell rung, and snoring. Ozzy and Francois talked across the room. A friendship seemed to be developing between them. Jimmy slept but Bull and Cowboy were playing cards. Did cowboys or farmers ever sleep? The Brits offered to take watch and sat near the tunnel with rifles. Lech sat by himself smoking still not entirely comfortable amongst the rest of us.

I felt like we had been lucky the first night against the Krauts in that pasture but tonight was a miracle. Well, I guess it was really Francois. Without him and his foresight, I wouldn't be here enjoying a quiet moment with his daughter. But the night would prove to be a turning point for us. The Germans were alerted to our presence and likely searching for us. There was no doubt that Americans had attacked that house but how many and from where they came, the Germans couldn't be sure.

"I am happy you are safe, Tony," Margaux said suddenly.

"Me too. It was touch and go there. Your father saved us. You should be proud of him," I said. Margaux looked at me over her shoulder.

"I am," was all she said. I stared into her pretty eyes. She was beautiful. Then she kissed me. Not a peck on the lips like before, but a real kiss. Wow!

"What was that for?" I asked.

"I like you," was all she said. She turned around and wiggled closer and I slipped my arms around her. Cowboy and Bull were staring at us, both of them with big grins on their faces.

"Shut up and play cards," I told them. Margaux laughed at all of us. I wasn't home and I wasn't with the rest of the 101st but for the time being, I was safe and things were good. That wouldn't last long, however. I didn't know it, but the next time I left this old cellar would be my last. For now, though, I was happy. As happy as a kid from New York who was dumb enough to join the Army Airborne could be. I fell asleep with Margaux in my arms, thinking of home and wondering if my mom would be mad if I married a French girl.

EPISODE 3 - INTO THE FIRE

I'd heard a guy back in England talking about war. He'd fought the Germans in Italy. He said something about war being a lot of sitting around, cleaning gear, playing cards and smoking interrupted by moments of sheer, absolute chaos. Something like that, anyway. I thought he was nuts. War was hell, right? Well, I changed my mind after yet another day of sitting in this old cellar bored out of my skull. It was D-Day plus six and I'd been in France for a week. During that time I'd seen my share of action, all of us had, but it amounted to about an hour's worth of battle.

Not that I was complaining, mind you. I much preferred the comfort of this resistance safe house to getting shot at but you could only check your gear and clean your rifle so many times. You could only play so many hands of poker. We couldn't even go out on patrol after our adventure two days past when we freed the two Brits, not to mention the Polish conscript Cowboy and I took prisoner that told us about the British prisoners in the first place. Francois, our Maquis contact, told us the place was crawling with Germans and they were looking specifically for American spies. I guess they were upset that Francois blew up their headquarters and we snatched two of the three Brits they were holding captive. The third was killed in the escape attempt.

"You are going to play or daydream about that French girl?" Cowboy asked, rousing me from my thoughts.

"If I had a pretty French gal hanging all over me, I'd be daydreaming about her too," Bull said defending me...sort of.

"I daydream about her anyway," Jimmy said crudely and they all laughed. Ozzy walked over and stood behind me. I thought he might jump in and tell them to lighten up. I should have known better.

"Tony, if you need a little time alone...,"Ozzy said leaving his thought unfinished. I just shook my head.

"You're all just jealous," I said as I threw down my cards to reveal my winning hand. "Three jacks! Read 'em and weep, you fucking hicks," I declared. Cowboy, Bull and Jimmy all groaned and tossed their hands away. Ozzy laughed and the Brits who were watching us play as they tried to remember how their Kraut machine pistols went back together joined in. Even Lech, the Polish conscript we'd found, seemed amused.

"He's fucking cheating," Jimmy cried out as I took the pot, a dozen Lucky Strikes. I don't know what he was complaining about. I gave them the damn smokes to begin with, a present from Margaux. As I put one of the smokes between my lips and fished out my Zippo, Francois appeared. He emerged from the tunnel that led from the old cellar with the sod covered roof that appeared to be just another part of the pasture above. It wasn't dusk yet and coming and going from the secret entrance was dangerous in daylight. Francois must have had something important to tell us to risk the hideout being discovered.

"Carentan has been captured!" Francois reported. He'd been feeding us information about the invasion, just general reports mostly from French civilians. It was good news. The 101st was in Carentan, or at least they were supposed to be, but that meant we were behind German lines with more and more Germans wedging themselves between us and the Allied forces every day. Even though it was good to hear, Francois didn't look happy.

"And you've got some bad news to go with that," Ozzy observed. Francois nodded.

"I am afraid so, my friend. The Nazis are moving to counter attack in force," Francois told us.

"Can't we do something about it?" Jimmy asked. James, the British Lieutenant, and Ember, his Scottish Sergeant, came and gathered around Francois.

"I'm afraid not, chap," James told him.

"He's right. That's likely to be a major battle, not a skirmish. We're talking maybe thousands of men, artillery, tanks and we'd have to wade through half the Krauts in France just to get there. That's why we're not there now," Ozzy agreed.

"I'm getting sick of hearing about all this stuff going on and we're not there to help," Bull announced. Cowboy nodded in agreement.

"Damn right," he added. Ozzy nodded slowly.

"Look, we all feel that way. I'd rather be in Carentan or wherever the 101st is but I'm not and we can't get there right now. We need to do what we can here and hope that sooner rather than later, an opportunity to link up presents itself," Ozzy told us. We all felt the same. As the days wore on and we heard more about the battles further north near the coast, the more frustrated we all felt.

"I may have something to occupy your minds in the meantime," Francois said. We all turned to regard the Frenchman. With the Germans patrolling the area heavily we had been stuck in the safe house and we all wanted to get out and make a difference. "There is a bridge that spans a canal. The American and English aircraft have not destroyed it and the Germans are moving equipment and men across it. From the air, it might look like nothing more than a small stone bridge but it is substantial,"

Francois reported.

"So we need to take it or destroy it?" Ozzy asked. James, even though he was a Lieutenant, deferred to Ozzy. I guess he figured Ozzy had things handled and knew a lot more about the situation. Maybe it was just because Ozzy and the rest of us had rescued him and Ember. Maybe he recognized, like the rest of us were beginning to, that Ozzy was one hell of a leader.

"My contacts tell me it needs to be destroyed. I volunteered to do so with your help. I have not made your presence widely known for fear of a mole but I insisted I would have it destroyed by tomorrow morning. You will help, won't you?" Francois told us. I think he knew we would but he asked anyway.

"We're itching to get out there and do something. I can't speak for the Brits or Lech, but the 101st will see it done," Ozzy said but Gene wasn't so eager.

"Hold on. We don't know anything about this bridge, how well it's defended or if we should even destroy it. With all due respect, Francois, how do we know your contacts are correct? The Allies could use that bridge as well once they break out from the coast," Gene argued. He had a point.

"You're right, Gene. Francois?" Ozzy replied and looked to Francois for more answers. Gene almost looked surprised Ozzy had so readily agreed with him. Usually they took their disagreements down the tunnel that led to the safe house. Gene wasn't insubordinate, but is seemed he felt it was his job to play devil's advocate.

"I have to agree, Francois. Ember and I will do whatever we can but we aren't fond of suicide missions. Save the one that got us into this mess in the first place," James added, referring to the invasion on D-Day and jumping behind enemy lines like we had.

"Fair enough. The bridge is lightly defended. My informants are in contact with others who speak with the commanders of the Allied army, or so I am told. We have explosives but we need cover...just in case," the Frenchman explained.

"England has made contact with the French and I suspect you Yanks have too. I also know the command in England sends radio signals with coded messages to the resistance and there is some communication beyond that also. Working with the locals is part of the strategy, is it not?" James offered. He was right. We had been instructed to make use of the local resistance, to use them for intelligence gathering, to locate the Germans and even fight alongside them if it made sense.

"I'm still of the mind that we do this. Look, if the Krauts are there and we can deny them passage, that can't be bad. The engineers can build a new bridge to replace this one if they need to and maybe we'll help the boys fighting in Carentan," Ozzy argued. James was right there with him.

"In my mind, denying Jerry movement now is more important," James added. The rest of us watched as if there was a tennis match going on, looking from Ozzy to James and now to Gene.

"Look, I'm not saying we shouldn't go. I just think we need to think it over, consider all the options, assess the risks. I want to kill those bastards as much as anyone, but I don't want to die for nothing," Gene said.

"I will go," Lech announced. "I agree that if there are Nazis, we should kill them. That is not nothing," he said. Gene wasn't fond of Nazis either. He was Jewish and had lost contact with distant relatives in Europe when the Nazis began their reign of terror. Lech, on the other hand, had suffered firsthand the brutality of the Nazis.

"Ozzy, we will go where you go. We owe you our freedom, if not our lives," James said and Ember nodded to indicate he agreed.

"Gene, you bring up some good points. I'm in charge and I know you support that but I respect your opinion too. What do you say?" Ozzy asked.

"Hell, I'm as anxious to do something as you are. Someone's got to keep you honest. I'm on board. If we can do the Nazi bastards some harm, we should do it. How about the rest of you?" Gene asked and looked around. He didn't get any negative answers from us.

"It's settled. When do we leave, Francois? We can be ready in an hour," Ozzy declared. We didn't have much beyond what we jumped with on D-Day and that had been gone through, sorted, packed and repacked half a dozen times.

"The bridge is some distance away. I will return before midnight with Henry, Margaux and some more men," Francois told us and I perked up. Margaux? She wasn't going, was she? I couldn't hold my tongue.

"Why is Margaux coming with us?" I asked.

"Tony, she is strong willed. I left her behind last time and she hasn't let me have a moment's peace since. As her father, I want to protect her too but even I can't stop her this time. I invite you to try. I know you are brave but I doubt even you are that brave," Francois said and then laughed. I should have known. She was sweet but I already knew Margaux had a stubborn streak too. She reminded me of my mom. I shook my head.

"I suppose you're right," I admitted.

"We'll look after her, Tony," Cowboy said and slapped me on the back. I nodded. I knew there was little I could do but I didn't have to like it and I meant to tell her when I saw her. Not that it would help but maybe it would make me feel better.

As Ozzy promised, we were ready to go an hour later. We were getting low on our own ammo so each of us had our M1 or Tommy gun as well as a German MP40 that we had pilfered from the German headquarters house when we rescued the Brits. Ozzy thought we might have to leave the Panzerschreck behind but Bull assured him he could carry it and a few of the rounds. Since the Brits and Lech didn't have weapons of their own, they only carried Kraut guns and extra ammo.

Lech wasn't allowed to go with us when we freed the Brits. We didn't know if we could trust him despite his story and willingness to help. But since the mission to free the Brits had gone well and his information had proven to be accurate, Ozzy, after talking it over with the rest of us, had decided to trust him. He still wore his Kraut uniform but he'd pulled off all the insignia. That helped a lot.

Ozzy went over our plan while we waited. Francois had shown us the bridge on the map and helped work out a plan of attack before he left. Henry and a small team of Maquis would handle the bridge. The rest of us, Francois and his daughter, the men of Baker Company, the Brits and the lone Pole would secure the area. The bridge sat near a 'T'-intersection. It crossed a canal that paralleled the main road that formed the top of that 'T' and the bridge sat on the side road that formed the tail. The main road was a more pleasant route, Francois assured us, but the side road was the more direct and the easier route for moving men and equipment.

We would secure the bridge that Francois assured us was guarded by only a handful of men while Henry and his small team would set the explosives. We were still behind enemy lines and there was no pressing need to hold a bridge like this with a major force, especially since the biggest threat was from the air. Preferably we would blow the bridge manually and then retreat but if needed, Henry had timed fuses too in case we couldn't blow the bridge manually. If we were lucky, we could all escape before the German's knew what hit them.

Yeah, right!

"Remember, short, controlled bursts when you switch to the MP40s. We've got a good supply of ammo, but we'll chew through that quick if we fire indiscriminately. I'll lead one team that will secure the bridge. Lieutenant Graham will lead another that will watch our flanks. Tony, Cowboy and Ember are with me. Jimmy, Gene and Bull are with James. Lech, you stick with me," Ozzy reminded us. I got the feeling that Ozzy wanted to keep an eye on Lech.

This operation was straight forward, or so we hoped. The plan, as always, was to get the job done without unnecessary risk or loss of life. I, for one, was glad to get out of the French safe house and do something. Engaging the enemy wasn't my idea of a good time but it beat sitting around thinking about it. I wasn't so worried about myself, however. It was Margaux that worried me. I'd seen her in action and I knew she could take care of herself but she just didn't look like a woman that should be out fighting a war. Hell, no woman, or man for that matter, should be fighting a war like this one.

We ate a light dinner and settled in to wait. I sat alone with my thoughts. I didn't think of home this time. I thought about Margaux. I'd only seen her once since the night we rescued the Brits but she was in my thoughts ever since. She was beautiful and I was drawn to her. I savored her touch and kisses. I was falling for the French girl. France was next to Italy. Maybe my mom wouldn't mind if I brought home a French girl instead of marrying an Italian girl from back home in Brooklyn.

"Tony, can I have a word?" Ozzy asked. I didn't even notice he had wandered over.

"Yeah, sure," I told him. He joined me on the crate I sat on.

"I'm not blind. I can see your sweet on that French girl. She's a beauty. But you need to keep your head about you. Don't do anything stupid. I need you to do your job, not fuss over that girl. She can take care of herself," Ozzy told me and then smiled warmly.

"I won't let you down," I told him.

"I know you won't. We'll all be looking out for each other. She'll be as safe as any of us," Ozzy said to reassure me. It didn't work.

"That's what I'm afraid of," I told him. Just then,

Francois and Margaux arrived. Ozzy slapped me on the shoulder and went to greet Francois. They had developed a friendship over the last week beyond the normal camaraderie that develops between men in trying times.

"Tony, don't say it," Margaux said as she came to me. Francois must have said something about my concerns but I played dumb.

"Say what?" I replied but I knew exactly what she meant.

"I can see it in your eyes. I am going tonight. I can take care of my...," was all Margaux was able to say before I grabbed her and kissed her. Her eyes flew open but closed as I pressed my lips to hers. I don't know why I did it. Maybe it was the prospect of dying or maybe I had deeper feelings for her I had yet to fully realize. In any case, it was nice and Margaux relaxed after a moment.

"I know," was all I said as I broke the kiss. Margaux blushed and that made her look even prettier.

"I'll be God damned," Cowboy muttered from across the room. Everyone was looking at us now but I didn't care.

"Tony, I...I will be careful. I promise," Margaux told me as she smiled up at me.

"If you two love birds are finished, we need to get going. Load up, we leave in five," Ozzy announced with his usual dry sense of humor. I turned to get my gear but Margaux stopped me and kissed my cheek. Fucking war! I guess I wouldn't have met her if it wasn't for the war but I knew there was no way we could really be together. Not for long anyway. That made all of this even worse.

A few minutes later, we were all exiting the hatch, two by two. The rest of the French, including Henry were stationed in the woods nearby looking for German patrols. Once we were all up top, we gathered and Francois translated Henry's report as we crouched amongst the trees.

"There is a patrol moving south. We should be able to

bypass them. The Nazis have set up a roadblock with machine guns on a road that lies on our path and we will need to go out of our way to avoid it. Henry suggests his team go ahead to scout and to make our presence less conspicuous. I suggest our two teams do that same. Each team can follow behind the team before it, staying close enough so we don't lose each other," Francois said.

"All right. Francois and Margaux are with me. James speaks French so we've got translators on each team. Besides, we need help to secure the bridge. James and his team should be small and mobile," Ozzy said. I was relieved that Margaux would be with me and I suspected Ozzy did that, at least in part, for my benefit. Henry and his team left us and a few moments later, James left with Jimmy, Bull and Gene keeping Henry and his team in view. Shortly after they left, Francois led our team out of cover and towards the bridge.

We picked our way, as usual, through cover and only exposed ourselves as necessary. It was slow going but it would help ensure we didn't get intercepted. We didn't see any Germans at first but that didn't last long. After we'd traveled for about half an hour, we ran into the back of Lieutenant Graham's team. They were crouched at the edge of a tree line looking ahead and waiting.

"What is it?" Ozzy whispered.

"Fritz is patrolling ahead. They narrowly missed Henry and his team. Now they have decided to take a smoke," James explained. Sure enough, a group of Krauts stood in a circle across a pasture, smoking and sharing a flask. I wish I had a flask of something stiff. We had a quarter moon but it was enough to clearly see the men if you were looking for them though their cigarettes were clearly visible glowing orange in the dark.

"We can wait them out, we can go around or we can attack," Ozzy offered quietly.

"Henry and his team will wait ahead and even if we lose them, I know the way," Francois told us suggesting we should wait. We waited for five minutes as the Krauts stood talking quietly, completely oblivious they were being watched by the enemy. Ozzy was clearly becoming frustrated. We had to blow that bridge before dawn. As luck would have it, a few moments later the Krauts all laughed as if someone had told a joke and then they split up and moved along.

We waited for the patrols to clear the area and James took his team ahead and a minute later we followed. We had a long way to go yet but we didn't encounter any more patrols along the way. Henry knew how to travel through the countryside to keep us well hidden. We sneaked along tree lines and hedgerows, through vegetable gardens and cow pastures. Only now and then did we cross a road and expose ourselves. The Krauts patrolled the roads rather than the maze of hedgerows and trees between them and we used that to our advantage.

Still, the trip made me nervous. There were over a dozen of us, split into three teams. If we were spotted, we were a long way from safety. It seemed, however, that Henry knew what he was doing. He lived here, probably grew up here, and knew the landscape like the back of his hand. No German, even after several years of occupation, knew Normandy like Henry did. Finally, after what seemed like the entire night, we arrived at the bridge without incident.

We gathered in a sparse grove of trees near the intersection. The paved main road running roughly east-west sat before us and a second gravel side road running north-south intersected it forming a 'T'. The bridge sat on the canal that paralleled off the main road. On the bridge, there were two sentries on each end. The plan was simple, take out the sentries, secure the area while Henry and his team set the explosives, blow the bridge and return to the safe house. If only it was really that simple.

"Our scouts tell me that there are less than a dozen men here. The four at the bridge along with four to six others that are camped in the trees beyond to relieve these men," Francois told us quietly. On the far side of the bridge, the side road ran north and disappeared amongst scattered trees a quarter mile beyond. Supposedly, that was the shorter route to get men and equipment to meet the Allied invasion. On the west of the side road, to our left, was an open field surrounded by trees. On the east side of that road, to our right, was a thick grove of trees, where the Germans camped. This area wasn't as heavily cultivated as much of the countryside was. It was dotted with open fields and small groves of trees along with the odd hedgerow, wall or fence.

"All right. The embankments of the roads and canal will give us good cover," Ozzy announced. The canal and the two roads offered embankments, more so to the east, which would afford us some protection on three sides. But we couldn't get there until the guards on the bridge were dispatched.

"Cowboy and Ember, you two take care of those guards...quietly. Tony, you go with them and watch their backs. James, take your team and find a good vantage point with good cover," Ozzy ordered. James and his team, Bull, Jimmy and Gene, were to provide cover and act as lookouts. On this side of the main road, an old stone wall paralleled the main road for about fifty yards opposite the bridge. It was crumbling in areas but would afford decent cover for James' team. Behind the wall was a field, the trees we were hidden in now and on the far side to the east a thick, overgrown hedgerow.

"And everyone, be careful. Let's get this done and get back to the safe house in one piece," Ozzy told us. Everyone nodded and then those of us with orders, moved out. James, Bull, Jimmy and Gene moved to spread out along the wall. Bull and Jimmy would man the Panzerschreck while Gene and James would act as lookouts. Cowboy, Ember and I moved off to the west to cross the road and make our way, hopefully undetected, to the bridge. The quarter moon provided enough light to see if you knew what you looking for but it wasn't so bright to expose us...or so we hoped.

The three of us managed to cross the road and creep within about thirty yards of the bridge. Cowboy and Ember had to take out those four sentries hand to hand. A gunshot would have alerted the other men camped nearby and would give them the chance to call in reinforcements. We didn't want to do this under fire. However, the reason for doing it was clear. Francois had told us the Allies were making gains and had secured a beachhead but this fight wasn't over yet. If we could slow the German advance, even a little, we had to do it. It was our job.

The three of us knew getting much closer was going to be difficult. I indicated I would remain behind and cover Cowboy and Ember. They set down their weapons and removed their helmets and then both men pulled their knives. The cowboy from Nevada and the man from Scotland advanced, crawling on their bellies. Three of the Kraut sentries were sitting on the stone walls that served as railings for the bridge. The forth, the one nearest to us, was standing as he smoked. None were especially alert. One might have even been sleeping. I'm sure they hadn't seen much action here and spent long hours with nothing to occupy their minds.

At ten yards out, the two Allies rose off the ground and closed the distance quickly. Ember was on the sentry that was smoking before he knew what hit him. The sentry on the other side of the bridge turned to look as Ember pulled the other man down the embankment but Cowboy was on him too quickly and took him to the ground on the far side of the road. Ember was already moving towards the other two sentries as Cowboy emerged and followed. His dull steel blade glistened with blood. One of the remaining sentries turned but Ember was on him, clamping his hand over the man's mouth and killing him quietly.

The other sentry stood in disbelief watching as his fellow soldier was killed. His shock lasted only a moment, however, before he turned to run. Cowboy gave chase as I leveled my rifle just in case. Firing a shot was preferable to the sentry reaching his unit and alerting them directly but I hoped I didn't have to pull the trigger. Cowboy was fast, however, and the sentry barely made it ten yards before Cowboy tackled him to the ground. The sentry tried to yell out, but even from my vantage point, I could tell the fall had taken his breath way. Cowboy made the condition permanent.

Still, I held my rifle ready just in case. When Cowboy finally crept back to the bridge and joined Ember, I lowered it. The two men crossed the bridge, gathered their gear and we moved to take positions on the far side of the road into the three-sided fortification formed by the embankments. We waited there, scouting the other side of the bridge. Two minutes passed and we didn't hear or see anything. The last sentry's half-hearted warning must not have reached the ears of his fellow soldiers camped somewhere in the trees across the canal.

We signaled for the rest of Ozzy's team, Francois, Margaux and Lech, along with Henry and his two fellow Frenchmen, that the coast was clear. They came two by two, Ozzy and Margaux bringing up the rear. Now all of us were huddled at the intersection of the two roads and the canal in the basin between the embankments. After a quick look around, Ozzy indicated to Henry and his men it was safe to do their work.

The three French men slipped over the embankment and down into the canal. They hardly made a sound as they began to go about rigging the bridge with their explosives. "Francois, Lech and I will take up positions along the side road. You take up position on the canal embankment. James and his team have our backs so focus to the north and east," Ozzy whispered and we did as he said. Margaux and I took up positions on the canal embankment near the bridge while Cowboy and Ember were about ten yards further to our right, Ember the last man on the line.

Things were going as planned and for a moment I thought we might pull this off. I looked over at Margaux and found her looking off beyond the canal. I wished she wasn't here but since she was, I was glad she was right next to me. Then a low whistle came from behind us. We all turned and saw Gene pointing off in the distance. Then we heard it. The groaning tracks told us immediately what it was. As I turned, a half-track appeared along the road beyond the bridge.

"Half-track!" I whispered harshly.

"We see it," Ozzy called back. Whether it was just a coincidence or the Krauts knew we were there didn't matter. We had to get this done and get it done quickly. Francois slipped over the embankment and informed Henry of our predicament. They traded words and then Francois slipped back amongst us.

"He needs time. It is a delicate thing they do," Francois told Ozzy.

"Well, we don't have a lot of time. If that thing spots us, we're dead," Ozzy said. He apparently assumed the half-track meant to cross the bridge. I wasn't so sure. Behind the armored vehicle were at least fifty men and as I watched, they began to deploy along the road and in the field off to the left. Lech saw it too.

"More soldiers and they are setting up defenses," the Pole told Ozzy. The half-track had stopped too, maybe a hundred yards beyond the bridge. Suddenly, the half-track's spotlight illuminated the bridge. We all got as low as we could. Did they know about us or were they wondering why no sentries guarded the bridge? Then men, maybe half a dozen, appeared from the trees across the canal and ran to the half-track. We watched this unfold, none of us sure they even knew we were there or what we were about.

"We're going to have to fight our way out of here," Ozzy warned, more a prediction than a statement born of any real knowledge.

"I can speak for Lieutenant Graham. If this must be done, we will see it though," Ember told Ozzy. Cowboy and I nodded.

"I will not leave my father and I know he will not leave," Margaux added. Francois looked at Ozzy and shrugged as if to say his daughter was correct. Ozzy looked back to where the others were hiding beyond the main road. I looked that way too but no one except Bull was visible. Even he was hidden in the shadows near the hedgerow and was nearly invisible unless you knew he was there. He clutched the Panzerschreck close to his body.

"All right. We'll hold those bastards off until Henry can rig the explo...," Ozzy began to say but as he spoke another half-track appeared behind him to the west along the main road. Its spotlight flared to life and swung around to light up the bridge too. Then suddenly its machine guns peppered the bridge with lead.

"Henry!" Margaux exclaimed as we all ducked. It was impossible to see what had become of Henry and his men since we were pressed low against the embankments that protected us. I could see where Bull had been hiding though and he was gone. The half-track's gun went silent as suddenly as they had come to life. Germans could be heard shouting beyond the canal.

"Cowboy, take a look and tell me what's happening," Ozzy said. None of us were sure the Krauts knew we were here yet. They obviously knew someone was threatening the bridge but they seemed focused on Henry and his team. Cowboy peered over the canal embankment with his eagle eyes and scanned the surroundings. Suddenly several bullets hit the embankment around him splashing him with dirt.

"Fuck! Two half-tracks, one to the west and one to the north. Maybe eighty men scattered beyond the canal.

Looks like some are moving to flank us to the east through those trees. Others are advancing on the canal," Cowboy said after he had taken cover.

"So, in other words, we're fucked," Ozzy spat.

"Pretty much and I'm guessing they know we're here," Cowboy replied as he brushed the dirt from his shoulders that erupted as the bullets had impacted the embankment.

"Hopefully those four are taking care of that half-track. Bull lugged that fucking cannon all the way here, I hope he plans on using it. Hold this position. Don't let those men flank us. They have to cross the canal and they'll be sitting ducks when they do. Otherwise, hold the Krauts off until Henry and his men are finished," Ozzy ordered us. He obviously assumed Henry and his men weren't dead already but we had no way of knowing.

The seven of us turned to face the advancing Germans, Ozzy, Francois and Lech facing west, the rest of us, Margaux, Cowboy and Ember, facing north. Suddenly, all hell broke loose. The half-track to the west on the main road erupted into a ball of smoke and flame. They might have known we were protecting the bridge but the Krauts apparently didn't know Bull and his Panzerschreck watched over us. If Henry and his men we still in the game, they could go to work without being hammered by machine gun fire. The other half-track didn't have the angle to reach them with its machine gun.

However, the telltale plume of acrid smoke from the Panzerschreck gave away Bull's position even in the darkness. The remaining half-track opened up tearing the trees behind the plume to shreds. The Kraut soldiers began firing on that location too. We took the opportunity to return fire catching half a dozen men in the open as they sought to gain the canal embankment. The four of us facing north cut two of them down but the rest made it to the opposite side of the canal.

"We can't hold them all off," Ember shouted. Another group of Krauts hit the bank on the opposite side of the bridge. Ozzy, Francois and Lech didn't have an angle and the Germans could fire on Henry and his men without being harassed. Then suddenly, the earth behind us beyond the main road erupted. Germans shouted commands in the field beyond the canal.

"Mortars!" Ozzy shouted. I looked over at Cowboy, but he was already moving to get a shot.

"They're going to walk those down right on top of us," I said.

"No. We are too close to the bridge. They obviously want it intact and I do not believe they will risk it," Francois explained.

"He's right. They want to silence Bull and his shoulder cannon," Ozzy agreed. We never stopped firing harassing shots as we discussed it.

"Your man Bull is why that half-track doesn't advance," Ember added. We kept the Germans on the far bank pinned down. If they were able to take out Bull, however, that half-track would advance and cut us to pieces.

"I got it!" Cowboy shouted as another mortar hit the trees behind us on the far side of the road. They were going to pepper that area with mortar fire in an attempt to keep the Panzerschreck silent or take it out altogether. Cowboy had moved down the embankment several yards and was lining up a shot.

"Keep those bastards across the canal quiet," Ozzy said. We were already firing at them to keep them from firing on Henry and his men but we intensified our fire. Then three potato mashers flew our direction. One hit the embankment and rolled into the canal. Another embedded into the bank above the canal but the last fell amongst us.

"Grenade!" I shouted. Ember rolled to the side. I scrambled to cover Margaux and shield her with my body. A moment later, the grenade went off. Suddenly my ears rang and I felt the rush of hot wind and a searing pain in my thigh. Margaux screamed. Dirt and gravel rained down on us. I rolled over and felt my thigh and my hand was covered in blood.

Tony!" Margaux called out but I didn't hear her. Suddenly all I could see was red. I scrambled to my feet and stood atop the embankment. I yanked a grenade from my suspenders, ripped the pin out with my teeth and threw it. Another followed that one. I vaguely heard bullets whiz by me, even felt the rush of air once or twice. The Krauts on the other bank scrambled to avoid the grenades and that's when I emptied the magazine of my M1.

Three men went down as they tried to avoid the grenades, the last one died when they went off. I stood on top of the embankment and switched to my MP40 and emptied the magazine down range on the Germans scattered about the field in front of me. I yelled something, riddled with slurs and curses as I took my sudden anger out on the Germans. Suddenly, someone grabbed my suspenders and yanked me off the embankment.

"Are you fucking daft, laddie?" Ember shouted as I came back to myself. I looked around and everyone was staring at me.

"Jesus, kid! Take it easy," Ozzy said with a hint of amusement in his voice. I was breathing hard and sweating. Margaux crawled next to me and looked at me concerned. Then she slapped me.

"Do not ever do that again," she said and then hugged me. I don't know what came over me. I guess being nearly killed by the grenade and Margaux being threatened too got the best of me. Margaux let me go and smiled at me. Something told me that French women were even more complicated than American women. She retrieved a cloth from the bag she carried and bound my leg. It wasn't bad, in other words I'd live, but it hurt like a son of a bitch. I watched her work, enjoying her touch, while the battle raged around us.

"It just cut you. I see no shrapnel," Margaux told me. That was good. Suddenly, Henry and his men scrambled up the embankment. As they topped it, one of Henry's men stiffened and fell back into the canal caught by a stray bullet. Another mortar hit the field behind us as more German's advanced on the canal. Henry and his remaining man settled amongst us, Henry speaking to Francois as his man took up a position next to Margaux to fire on the advancing soldiers. Cowboy was lining up another shot on the mortar team having missed his previous opportunity. The rest of us returned fire to keep the Krauts pinned down.

"Henry says the explosives are set," Francois translated. Ozzy turned and signaled the team behind us, though he probably had no idea where they were. Another mortar round landed, this time short and on the road just behind us. We all took cover as debris rained down on us. Then we heard the searing hiss of a rocket. I looked up and watched the missile sail over our heads and explode in the field across the canal. Those things were meant for penetrating armor but they would work against men too.

"Mortar team down!" Cowboy shouted. The half-track and what sounded like every Kraut opened up on the position from where the Panzerschreck had fired. I hoped Bull and the others had moved and quickly. Suddenly, we heard footsteps to the east and out of the gloom, Bull and his Panzerschreck appeared followed by James, Gene and Jimmy. They all but jumped amongst us to avoid the barrage of fire.

"You get that damned bridge ready to blow yet?" Bull asked as he flopped down amongst us.

"Nice work with that cannon," Ozzy commented and then asked, "How do we get out of here?"

"We're clear to the east. If we go in small groups and then blow the bridge, we can escape. We don't have much time. The sky in the east is already light," James announced. Sure enough, we didn't have long before the dawn would make our escape difficult at best. Francois translated for the Frenchmen as most of us fired on the

Germans to keep them honest. We weren't going to win this battle but we could keep them off of us long enough to escape.

"Henry and his man will stay to blow the bridge and then slip away into the night. They blend in better than you," Francois said. That was an understatement.

"You've had quite a go of it down here. My team will cover your escape and follow behind once you're clear," James told us.

"Yeah, luckily that mortar team couldn't hit the broadside of a battleship," Gene remarked.

"Thanks! Get ready to...," Ozzy started to order when bullets hit the ground. "Get down!" Ozzy yelled. We hit the ground and heard men shouting in German behind us. The men we'd seen disappear into the trees had reached the canal, maybe fifty yards east of our position. We never saw them. Those of us that could returned fire. Against the canal embankment we had good cover but so did the Krauts. Time was running out and our escape had been cut off. There was no way we could all sneak past those men that had appeared out of the trees.

Krauts were gaining the far bank of the canal on both sides of the bridge now. We had cover but it wouldn't last for long and we just didn't have enough firepower to hold them off. At some point we would be overwhelmed unless we left soon but there was nowhere to go that wouldn't get half of us killed. Even the half-track that had held back to avoid the Panzerschreck was moving into position to fire on us.

"Blow the damn thing!" Ozzy shouted.

"Are you sure?" Gene asked. Francois hesitated to give the order to Henry.

"The only chance we have is to blow the bridge and use the distraction to escape," Ozzy told him.

"We're dead if we stay," James added. Just then, Krauts appeared on our side of the canal on the other side of the bridge. Lech and Francois killed them, but others were right behind them.

"We're dead either way. This is a suicide mission now. Blow it," Gene agreed. Ozzy nodded at Francois and he relayed the order to Henry. I looked at Margaux, bullets flying over our heads. She smiled wistfully at me. This wasn't how we'd planned this mission. We were supposed to get in and get out quickly but the Krauts had either been alerted to our presence or the intelligence Francois had was inaccurate. In any case, this operation was doomed from the start.

"We came here to blow this bridge. We might save a lot of lives, American, British and French by slowing these bastards down just a little. Maybe not. But it's what we came to do. We all knew death was a possibility. If we're destined to die here, let's take a lot of these bastards with us," Ozzy announced. It was a solemn statement but somehow it gave us courage.

"I think I speak for all of us. It's been a pleasure. I'm proud to die amongst heroes," James said. Ozzy nodded and we all took cover. I held Margaux close, covering her head. Henry triggered the explosives and...nothing. Henry shouted, clearly cussing up a storm in French.

"The Nazis that crossed the canal must have found the explosives," Francois said.

"Shit! I'm not going to die here for nothing," Ozzy said. He switched to his MP40. Henry and his man moved to join him. They seemed to understand his intent.

"We'll cover you," Gene said, apparently knowing Ozzy's mind too.

"You men, get some fire on those men to the east. Bull, put your last round on those men that crossed the canal," James ordered. We all moved without hesitation.

"I will go with you," Lech told Ozzy. It wasn't really a request. Ozzy nodded. Bull moved to a get bead on the men that were manning the canal beyond the bridge. Ember, Cowboy and I fired on the men to the east across the canal to let Bull get off a shot and let Ozzy, Lech and the Frenchmen get down into the canal. We let the Krauts have it. Francois and Margaux, along with Gene and Jimmy, pinned down the men on the far side of the bridge.

"Go!" James shouted. Ozzy, Lech and the two Frenchmen slipped over the embankment and rolled down into the canal. They came up firing. Ozzy shouted orders to Lech as they moved under the bridge. We couldn't see it but there was a vicious fire fight under the bridge. Bull took the opportunity to not just line up a shot with his Panzerschreck but to climb onto the road and then the bridge. Bullets shattered the stone all around him as he poked the weapon over the stone railing and fired at the krauts that had flanked us. The rocket exploded and Bull dashed back to cover amongst us leaving the tube behind. He didn't have any more ammo anyway. The half-track must've seen that and moved forward, it's machine gun firing a steady stream of lead on our position. Suddenly, Ozzy rolled over the embankment on the far side of the bridge. Lech was right behind him. They crawled quickly along the embankment. Then Henry and the other Frenchman appeared.

The bridge exploded suddenly. Henry fell over the embankment as his fellow Frenchman was thrown broken and bloody several yards. Everyone took cover as stones and rubble showered us. Margaux screamed. I looked up and the bridge wasn't completely destroyed but it was unusable. The middle section had dropped into the canal and the abutments were cracked and broken. Unfortunately, without the bridge to protect, the half-track advanced and another mortar team let loose.

Machine gun fire whistled over our heads and a mortar fell in the canal giving us a much needed shower. Henry struggled to his knees and was cut down by the machine gun but now we could all see the explosion had already done him in. "Henry!" Margaux shouted and began to go to him. I grabbed her and held her from going.

"You'll be killed," I told her. She struggled for a

moment but then gave up crying. I wished I could have held her, but I had work to do. The sky was bright in the east now. Escape, even if we weren't surrounded, would have been difficult. But the Germans had all of our escape routes covered. Another mortar round landed on the road behind us and once again we were showered with rubble. Something told me the next mortar round would split the difference and kill us all.

"Cowboy!" Ozzy shouted from across the road using the bridge for cover. Cowboy was way ahead of him. Ember covered him as he tried to find the mortar team. It was hard. The air was filled with smoke. We might have used it for cover but the hail of bullets flying over our heads would have cut us down as we emerged from cover. The Krauts had no such problems. We couldn't put enough fire on them to keep them from advancing. The canal served as a barrier of sorts but eventually the mortars would find us or the Krauts would get close enough to get grenades on us.

"Hold them back," James told us. We were doing all we could but it wasn't enough. Another mortar fell and this one landed just past Ozzy and Lech. For a moment, I thought they were goners but as the smoke cleared, both had avoided major injury. Lech's face was bloody but Ozzy was untouched. I was beginning to wonder if he was Superman. I don't think he'd been injured at all since we landed in France, not even a scratch.

Now the half-track had come as close as it could to the bridge with mortars falling, or rather what was left of the bridge. Its machine gun still didn't have the angle to get to us but it effectively kept us pinned down. We were truly trapped now. Another mortar came down and hit the opposite side of the embankment we took cover behind. The heat and pressure surged up and over the bank but we were spared the brunt of its deadly force.

"Fuck! I can't find the mortar team with all this smoke," Cowboy shouted.

"It doesn't really matter. It's not going to make a difference at this point," Ember told him. Grenades came from the east and I managed to kill one of the men that tossed them. The potato mashers fell short and exploded harmlessly in the canal. I took the opportunity to look back at Margaux. Damn, I didn't mind dying so much but I didn't want her to die. She deserved to live but I couldn't do a damn thing about it. The sun peaked over the horizon as I looked at her and then her eyes went wide.

"What?" I asked and looked over my shoulder. As I did, two planes roared overhead and the half-track went up in a ball of fire. The two fighters, P-47 Thunderbolts, soared over the field beyond the canal and one peeled off to the left as the other went right. The Krauts were suddenly in a panic. One of the fighters made a tight turn and came back for another run, this time using its .50 caliber machine guns. The ground erupted before the fighter and Germans died by the dozens.

The second Thunderbolt came around from the southeast and roared overhead tearing into the Germans in the trees across the canal before firing its rockets on the men running for cover in the field. I almost felt bad for the bastards. The other fighter roared over the field and dropped one of its five-hundred pounders amongst the Germans. All of us were up and watching the fireworks. None of the Krauts had the wherewithal to stay put and fire on us any longer.

"Fuck yeah!" Bull shouted. Gene was on his knees, eyes closed looking to the heavens. Ozzy and Lech were both picking off survivors across the canal as they retreated from the hell being unleashed from above. Cowboy and Ember were doing the same. Jimmy was kissing the cross he wore around his neck. Margaux threw her arms around me. The second P-47 took a wide turn and came back towards us just over the tops of the trees waggling its wings at us. Francois wiped a tear from his eye as James shook his hand.

The Krauts had been routed but many had survived and managed to retreat. They would be back, however. The other Thunderbolt joined the one that flew over us and they disappeared the way they had come. "Get your asses in gear. Those fuckers will be back and sooner rather than later," Ozzy yelled. As if on cue, several troops emerged from the far side of the field. They didn't look happy.

"Come on, we need to go now!" Ozzy said as he climbed to his feet. Most of us were already getting ready to go. Those of us still using M1s or Tommy guns abandoning them in favor of the MP40s we carried to save weight. Seconds later, we all were ready to go. "Which way, Francois?" Ozzy asked.

"There is a place nearby we can use," Francois replied.

"Lead on. Heads down, move fast, don't fall behind!" Ozzy announced. James ensured everyone was up and moving and then took up the rear as Ozzy followed Francois. My leg hurt but I was just happy to be out of that gully that almost served as our graves. We dashed across the road and the Krauts were already firing at us. They seemed intent on extracting some revenge but there weren't enough of them to hold us there. We left the road and made our way through the fields, along hedgerows and tree lines, towards places unknown as quickly as we could. Margaux was just ahead of me.

"Where are we going?" I asked.

"I am not sure. Some place safe I hope," she replied. We heard shots behind us as we made our way, crouched low and running.

"I'm sorry about Henry," I told her.

"He was a good man. He's with his wife and child now," Margaux told me. That thought really irked me. I knew they were waiting for him because of the fucking Krauts. Germans were pursuing us, shouting orders and firing seemingly indiscriminately.

"Did you see those Krauts?" Jimmy whispered from

behind me.

"What about them?" I asked.

"SS, Tony. Those are SS troops behind us," Jimmy told me. I looked back over my shoulder as I ran. Ember was right behind him and nodded.

"Afraid so, laddie," he told me. That made my blood run cold. We encountered SS troops a week before when we destroyed the two eighty-eights but we didn't know it at the time. The SS was like the boogie man. Just mentioning them was enough to make a grown man shake with fear. Little did I know the SS in Carentan were learning that the 101st Airborne was even more frightening.

We moved through the woods as quickly as we could without making a racket. As we approached the edge of the trees we were moving through, a Kraut troop transport rolled by followed my two motorcycles. They didn't see us but it was close. If they went by a moment later, they would have caught us on the road. We waited until they were gone from sight and then crossed the road. On the far side, set back in the trees, we found an old barn that was partially collapsed. Francois led us inside and then he opened a hatch in the wooden floor with stairs leading down. I'd never have noticed it if Francois hadn't opened the hatch.

Once we were all inside, Francois closed the door behind us. The room was dark, musty and cramped, but it was safe for the time being. "I apologize for the conditions. We did not build this but found it by chance. It serves us well in emergencies such as this," the Frenchman said.

"It's hidden from Jerry and so it's perfect," James commented.

"I agree. Like a five-star hotel," Ozzy said.

"Margaux and I will keep watch from the loft above. I will whistle if we are discovered. Otherwise, stay here until night falls. If you hear my whistle, you come out shooting," Francois informed us.

"We will not let anyone find you," Margaux added and I wondered what that meant. I hoped she wasn't going to do something stupid. They cautiously climbed from the hole in the ground we found ourselves in. Margaux turned to look at me as she exited and blew me a kiss. As soon as she was gone, Cowboy elbowed me in the ribs grinning. I just smiled back. It struck me how quickly we could go from near death to joking around again.

"Out of the frying pan, so to speak," James remarked.

"We're lucky to be alive. I'll take this hole over that bridge any day of the week," Ozzy replied quietly.

"Thank God for those flyboys," Gene said.

"You think they know something? Maybe they were looking for us," Jimmy wondered.

"No, they likely saw the smoke from the bridge or the mortar blasts and found a bunch of easy targets," Ozzy told us. He was probably right. As far as anyone knew, we were dead and unaccounted for. The U.S. Army wasn't going to search for a missing stick of paratroopers. I saw several other transports get hit and go down as we flew over the coast. There were probably hundreds of missing men and we were just six more. Same with the Brits. They were probably assumed dead too.

"Do you think they might report seeing us? They did acknowledge us," Ember said referring to the Thunderbolt that flew over us waving its wings.

"Could be but they're likely out of England. By the time that news reaches our boys over here in France, the war might be over," James said. We all laughed softly. Hell, that news might never get to France with all the channels and chains of command. "Well, what now?" James asked.

"I was just thinking about that," Ozzy answered.

"So, you going to let us in on your thoughts?" Gene asked.

"Well, if Francois is right and the 101st is in Carentan, we're likely as close to them as we are to the safe house," Ozzy said.

"But there's half the Kraut army between us and them," I reminded him. James turned to regard me.

"I'm afraid we've stirred up a hornet's nest. Jerry's everywhere and they are on alert. Going back to the safe house is likely as dangerous as going forward. Not to mention it takes us further from our brothers in arms," James explained. What all that meant for me, I didn't grasp just yet.

"I'm up for breaking through. I'll miss the Frenchie's food but I want to find the rest of Baker Company," Bull said.

"I agree. It's time to go home, or as close as we can get anyway," Gene agreed.

"Any objections?" Ozzy asked. No one said a word. I think we all wanted for this little adventure to be over. "What about you Tony? Can you leave that pretty French girl behind?" Ozzy asked and I looked up at him.

"They ain't coming with us?" I asked.

"I can't ask them to come with us. You don't want Margaux fighting her way through the lines, do you? Besides, they live here," Ozzy told me.

"She'll be safer here, laddie," Ember said and Cowboy put his arm over my shoulders.

"This is my second family. I go where you go. You're right, she's safer here," I said fighting back tears. I hadn't even considered having to leave her at some point. I knew I'd have to eventually but I hadn't thought about it.

"The Allied army will devour the Nazis and you will be reunited soon enough," Lech offered. He didn't speak much, always staying apart from the rest of us. But maybe after the battle at the bridge, he felt more like one of us.

"From your lips to God's ears," Gene said.

"Amen," Ozzy added. "So, after dark we head north, towards Carentan. I wish I could guarantee we'll all make it but I can't. We've been lucky up until now and maybe heaven's looking down on us, but we've got a lot of those Kraut devils to get through," Ozzy said solemnly. Nobody spoke after that. Instead we all withdrew into our own thoughts. Ozzy forbade us from smoking because of the odor. I wished I chewed tobacco like Cowboy and Bull right about then. I wished Margaux was down here with me too.

The days were long and the nights short in France during the month of June. We had many hours of boredom ahead of us but we couldn't do much to keep our minds occupied. As I sat there with my own thoughts, I wondered about those planes and how they came to find us. It was better than thinking about leaving Margaux. We'd gotten a lot of breaks, getting out of that transport on D-Day not being the least of them. Maybe we had something more important to do. Maybe God really was on our side.

Years later, I found out at a 101st Airborne reunion how those flyboys had come to save our asses. A man approached me and asked me point blank about that day. I was surprised and asked him how he knew. He wasn't wearing the 101st insignia, instead wearing a jacket with insignia from the 56th fighter group. He told me he'd been searching for the men he saw from the air that day since the war ended. We spent hours talking about it. I told him how the men of Baker Company came to be there, our little adventure behind enemy lines.

He told me he and his fellow pilot saw the smoke and came to investigate. They were giddy when they saw the Germans out in the open like that and tore into them. Neither of them could figure out why Americans were that far behind the lines or how we managed to hold off that many Germans. Even though he had been searching for us for almost two decades, no one seemed to know much about what we'd done. It took him that long to finally track me down. I told him he saved our asses that day and thanked him. It made him happy to hear that. However, sitting in that hole in the ground under that collapsed barn,

I was just glad those flyboys had found us.

Hungry and tired, we all tried to catch a little shuteye during the day. Even I managed to sleep a little despite the thought of leaving Margaux behind weighing heavy on my heart. Maybe it was the war or the fact I'd stared death in the face so many times over the last week, but I loved that girl. I promised myself I was going to marry her if I survived the damn war. My mom would have to give up on me marrying some local Italian girl.

Our little hole was almost pitch black when Francois finally came to get us. He reported that he and Margaux had seen many Germans, including SS, scouring the area but they largely ignored the partially collapsed barn. I admit it didn't look like a place that could hide all of us and they had a lot of ground to search. We all climbed out of the hole, our muscles cramped and aching. We immediately moved to a dense patch of trees to discuss our next move.

"The safe house is several kilom...," Francois began to say but Ozzy didn't let him finish.

"We're not going back, Francois," Ozzy informed him. Margaux gasped.

"Where will you go?" Francois asked.

"We've decided to try to link up with our units. If what you tell us is right, they're not much further away than that old cellar. We'd love to oblige ourselves of your hospitality a while longer but we're a liability to you and the Maquis. We'll likely have as much trouble going back as we would going forward. Besides, you and your daughter can blend in. We can't," Ozzy explained. Francois looked pained but not nearly as much as Margaux who wouldn't even look at me.

"I don't know what to say, my friend. We've been through much together and in such a short time. I am sad to see you go but I understand," Francois told Ozzy and reached out to shake his hand. Margaux was crying softly and finally she looked at me.

"Ozzy?" I asked and he looked at me. I could see he understood.

"Just be careful," he whispered. I took Margaux's hand and led her aside. We moved several yards away through the trees and when I stopped, she hugged me tightly.

"I'm sorry. I have to do this," I told her.

"I know," was all she said as I pulled her close and squeezed.

"I love you, Margaux," I told her and she pulled away and stared into my eyes. She smiled through her tears.

"I love you too. Please be careful. I can't bear the thought of...," she said, leaving the unpleasant thought unsaid.

"I'm going to come back and marry you. I promise," I told her and she welled up again but this time her eyes were joyful. Then she kissed me. Ozzy and Francois approached and we parted.

"It's time, kid. You take care of yourself, Margaux. I'll take care of Tony," Ozzy told her as Margaux let go of me and hugged Ozzy. Francois looked as if he might cry himself and took my hand and shook it.

"Come back to us. Both of you," Francois said.

"We will," I told them. I took Margaux's hand one last time and then Ozzy and I turned and left as Margaux's hand slipped from mine. I couldn't bring myself to look back. If I did, I might have deserted.

"I better get an invite to the wedding," Ozzy said to distract me.

"Hell, if we both make it you're my best man," I told him.

"Deal, kid!" he replied and we joined the others.

We moved out, quietly. Before we left, we dumped everything we didn't need back in the trees. If it wasn't for killing, it didn't come along for the journey. We'd eaten most of our K-rations in that hole during the day. Francois had given Ozzy a rough idea of what lay in front of us and what to avoid. More than anything, we just had to stay hidden and move north. If we were lucky, we'd slip through the lines and find the rest of the 101st by morning.

Good luck! Nothing in my experience so far told me that was likely to happen. This wasn't going to be easy. My gut told me so. For an hour we moved from one bit of cover to the next. We were flying blind, however, without Francois there to lead us. Even Lech wasn't familiar with this part of Normandy. So we just pushed on, slowly and methodically, each step taking us closer to our goal and likely closer to danger too.

"Hold!" Ozzy whispered harshly. We all dropped into crouches as Ozzy and James conferred. They were checking the compass. "We need to go back," Ozzy told us. No one questioned him. We backtracked a quarter mile and there Ozzy pulled us together. "There's a village or a cluster of farmhouses ahead. I could see water too. Ponds or flooded fields. We'll need to go around," he told us. No one replied.

We set out again, this time westerly. It was slow going and I was beginning to have doubts we could do this before dawn. I didn't want to spend another day hiding out, especially without good cover. Jimmy was on point, with Ozzy right behind working the compass and keeping us on track. Suddenly, Ember, who was behind Jimmy, Ozzy and Lech, stopped the rest of us by raising a clenched fist. We stopped and crouched and Ember was able to grab Lech and stop him too. A moment later, we all found out what the problem was.

Jimmy stopped at the edge of the hedgerow we were creeping along and stumbled right on top of a Kraut patrol. At first, neither Jimmy nor the handful of Germans was sure what was going on but then one of the Krauts shouted, "Amerikaner!" That wasn't good.

A shot rang out and Jimmy slumped to the ground. Ozzy's MP40 lit up the early morning sky and the

Germans all fell dead but more were already on their way. Ember turned and waved us off with a hand as bullets began to fly. Cowboy, Bull, and I managed to make a break for it but the rest of them were quickly surrounded. We found a break in the hedgerow and sneaked through to the far side. As we did, a staff car pulled up to the scene. We couldn't see what was happening very well but we could hear.

"Well, well, it looks like we've caught our spies," came a harsh voice with a thick German accent. "And it appears we've recaptured our English prisoners as well," the Kraut announced, an officer I assumed. A troop transport pulled up and we could hear boots hit the ground. "Take them away and search the area for others," the German said and we heard Krauts begin to move our way as their flashlights lit up the night and what sounded like dogs scoured the area. The three of us looked at one another and moved off in the other direction as everyone else was loaded onto the truck and we heard it drive away.

EPISODE 4 - THE ROAD HOME

The three of us, Cowboy, Bull, and I, had moved off a couple of hundred yards from the fray. We could see Krauts searching the woods with dogs and flashlights coming our way. I don't think any of us knew what to do. Everyone else, the two Brits, Lech, Gene and Ozzy, had been captured as far as we knew. I was pretty sure Jimmy had been shot but whether or not he was dead I couldn't know. I didn't have time to ponder it, however. We'd be dead soon if we weren't careful. I was in the lead and when we reached a dense stand of trees, I stopped to face the other guys.

"Holy shit! What do we do?" Bull asked.

"I don't know," I replied.

"We should get out of here before those Krauts find our trail," Cowboy added.

"And leave everyone else behind?" I asked.

"We don't even know where they're being taken," Bull interjected.

"I bet they're headed towards the town Ozzy saw before we back tracked," Cowboy surmised. He was probably right.

"Well, let's head there and see what's what. The Krauts

probably won't be expecting that," I said. We all agreed and turned to head in that general direction. Suddenly, someone loomed up in front of us. We all raised our weapons but it was Cowboy and his eagle eyes that called us off.

"Ozzy!" Cowboy said as he signaled us to stand down.

"We can cut through these trees and head off that truck if we hurry," Ozzy announced.

"How the hell did you...," Bull began to ask but Ozzy cut him off.

"Later. Let's go!" Ozzy whispered harshly. Ozzy took off towards the small village we had tried to navigate around when everything went so wrong. We were running, low and fast. "Get your weapons ready," Ozzy hissed over his shoulder. We had all abandoned our M1s back at the bridge and had switched to the Kraut machine pistols we took from the German headquarters when we rescued the Brits. We checked ammo as we ran.

Suddenly, Ozzy skid to a stop and we stopped and stood next to him. We found ourselves at the edge of a road. Twenty yards to our left was a guard shack and two guards. One stood as the other sat on a stool, both were smoking and talking. "That truck will be coming any moment," Ozzy told us. "I'll take care of those guards. You three wait just past the guard shack. The staff car with Field Marshal Von Dusseldorf in it is right behind the truck. Bull, you take care of the guards in the back of the truck. You two relieve Dusseldorf of his fancy car. We're going to drive to Carentan," he ordered and turned to go.

Field Marshal Von Dusseldorf? Even in situations like this, Ozzy's wry sense of humor was there. The three of us did as Ozzy ordered, moving through the trees to where the truck would stop for the guards. I guess they'd be stopping for Ozzy instead of the regular guards, however. We got in position and watched as Ozzy took care of business. He walked out of the trees casually and approached the guards like he'd known them all his life.

"Cigarette?" Ozzy asked with a horrible German accent.

One guard dug through his pockets looking for a smoke but the other man was catching on. He went for his rifle but Ozzy's machine pistol hit him across the jaw and the man crumpled to the ground. The other guard was caught completely by surprise and I wasn't sure he knew what exactly was happening even when Ozzy stuck his knife in the man's heart. He tried to scream but it was more of a soft groan as Ozzy laid him down on the road. Suddenly, the truck rounded the bend in the road, the staff car right behind it.

Ozzy hurriedly shoved the two dead men into the guard shack and reappeared as he slipped into one of their jackets and donned a Kraut helmet just as the truck stopped. Apparently the driver expected to be checked before being allowed to proceed and followed protocol. The truck, with its hooded headlights, didn't cast enough light on Ozzy to reveal he was an imposter. Ozzy walked up to the driver's door as the truck waited and then pointed his MP40 at the driver. "Out!" was all he said. The German officer seated in the topless staff car stood up and shouted something in German. That's when Cowboy and I rushed the car and Bull went to the back of the truck.

The officer went for his sidearm, but Cowboy shoved the barrel of his MP40 in the man's ribs. "I don't think so Dusseldorf," he said. The Kraut officer glared menacingly at Cowboy as he was relieved of his sidearm. I roughly helped the driver out of his seat and made him lie on the ground. I took his sidearm, a Lugar, and found his MP40 on the seat next to him. The other guys would need those.

While Cowboy helped the officer out of the car, Bull waited at the back of the truck. A guard poked his head out of the canvas cover to see what was going on and Bull reached up, yanked him from the truck and threw him on the ground like he was a rag doll. Bull stomped on the man's neck and then the other guard flew out on his own, the other guys apparently in on the impromptu rescue now. That guard was quick, however, and got to his feet, fists in the air as Bull approached.

"You will not escape. In fact, your pitiful invasion will be repelled and the Reich will push you back into the Atlantic," the officer said. A true believer.

"Shut up, Dusseldorf," Cowboy replied. The Field Marshal scowled at him like my mom used to look at me when I screwed up.

Ozzy had the driver out of the truck, pulled the kraut helmet off his head and hit the driver across the face with it. The man went down like a sack of potatoes. Ozzy slipped out of the German coat and retrieved his own helmet. "Quit fucking around. Let's go!" he told us harshly. The German guard hit Bull in the jaw but the big man from Oklahoma just laughed and punched the man in the gut. He doubled over and fell to the ground. Bull kicked him in the side and then gathered the guard's weapons and ammo.

"Been a pleasure, Field Marshal," I told the officer. He could have been a real field marshal for all I knew but who really cared? He stared at me with obvious contempt but a moment later, Cowboy slammed the butt of his machine pistol into the back of the officer's skull. Suddenly, Von Dusseldorf wasn't so smug. I punched the nervous driver sending him to the pavement and then shook the pain from my hand. "Get in, Cowboy!" I said as I climbed into the driver's seat.

Ozzy climbed into the cab of the transport as Bull handed the weapons to someone in the back of the truck and climbed in himself. A moment later the truck lurched ahead, gears grinding. Apparently, those things weren't meant for speed. I swerved around the two guards lying on the road that Bull had dispatched and we headed slowly towards the small village beyond but at the first crossroad, Ozzy went left.

"Is this the right way?" I asked Cowboy.

"I have no idea where we are anymore with all these

fucking trees," he said.

"I hope Ozzy does," I told him. We drove down the road but that truck had a top speed of about thirty-five miles an hour. Either that or Ozzy didn't know how to drive the damn thing. Suddenly, the truck shuddered to a stop. I looked at Cowboy and he seemed to understand. We could see the moon now and Cowboy informed me we were headed south, away from Carentan. The truck backed up to turn around. I drove the staff car around the truck, turned around and followed Ozzy back the way we had just come. This place was like a maze.

As we approached the intersection, a halftrack pulled across the road to block our way. They knew what was up. Ozzy stopped the truck but I had other plans. "What the fuck are you doing?" Cowboy asked as I accelerated and sped around the truck. I pointed the car right at the half-track. Its machine gun opened up and bullets rang off the front end of the fancy car as Cowboy and I ducked low.

"Jump!" I shouted. Cowboy looked at me like I was crazy but he went for his door. Cowboy and I opened our doors and dove out of the staff car after I grabbed the extra MP40. I rolled to a stop on the pavement but Cowboy was already on his feet. We watched as the car slammed into the halftrack. For a moment, we weren't sure the car had done much damage to the armored vehicle but then both exploded and lit up the night.

"Warn me before you play chicken," Cowboy told me a mix of anger and amusement on his face. I laughed at him. I was feeling pretty full of myself after the rescue but before I could gloat, the truck pulled up between us.

"Get in!" Ozzy ordered as he threw open the passenger door. Cowboy and I piled into the cab as Ozzy coaxed the transport forward. He reached into his shirt and pulled out our map. "Figure out where the fuck we are," he said tossing the map at us as we drove around the burning half-track and went right, back the way we had come. We drove past the guard shack, but Dusseldorf was gone. Then two motorcycles raced up behind us. If we were going to drive to Carentan, we were going to do it with a Kraut escort.

Suddenly, we heard gunfire and one of the motorcycles went down sending a fountain of sparks trailing behind it. More gunfire and the other motorcycle veered off the road and into a ditch. "Glad to see they aren't napping back there," Ozzy observed.

"How the fuck did you not get captured? You were right behind Jimmy," I asked.

"Ember. He yanked me aside and threw me to the ground. In the confusion, I guess they didn't see me. I wedged myself under that hedgerow. The dogs ignored me. The whole area was covered in scent. Then I slipped through the hedge and saw you three idiots," Ozzy explained.

"You are fucking Superman," I told him. Ozzy laughed.

"Just find where we are on the map," he replied but I could see the smile on his face. Suddenly an armored car pulled out onto the road in front of us. Its machine gun blazing as it sped towards us. "Get down!" Ozzy yelled but he didn't have to. Cowboy and I were already ducking. Ozzy stepped on the gas as he peeked over the dashboard. We would probably win if we collided with the armored car, or rather the truck would. We'd be mincemeat. Ozzy didn't slow or turn, though. I dared to look as the armored car raced towards us and cringed.

At the last moment, the car veered and rolled onto its side as Ozzy sat up again. "They must have radios. They know about us," Ozzy said. My heart was pounding. Cowboy had a death grip on the dashboard. I don't think he liked playing chicken. Ozzy, on the other hand, was calmly considering the situation as if we were sitting around back in England drinking beer.

"Signpost!" Cowboy shouted as we got ourselves upright again, sharing the passenger seat. Ozzy slowed enough to let us read it. Good luck! It was just a blur to me but Cowboy could read it. Well, he could see it, anyway.

"I can't even pronounce that," Cowboy complained.

"Just find it on the map," Ozzy told him. We rumbled down the road, alone for the moment. Cowboy searched the map trying to find the name we'd seen on the sign. Then he pointed to a spot.

"Got it!" I announced. "Fuck! This road turns south and I don't see any major crossroads for miles," I told Ozzy.

"Why not? Let's not make this easy for once," he said sarcastically and turned the truck around. We went back the way we'd come, retracing our steps once again.

"It's go through that village or go south, Ozzy," Cowboy announced.

"Shit and this truck is a pig! We'll never outrun anyone and we can't drive around on these roads all night trying to find a way to Carentan," he said just as two more armored cars came around the bend ahead and more headlights appeared behind us. "Hold on!" Ozzy said as he cranked the wheel and turned right on to a narrow gravel road lined with hedgerows and trees. It was full of ruts and we could hear a couple of carefully chosen words shouted from the back of the truck.

The armored cars followed us down the winding road, their machine guns firing wildly but not hitting much of anything. "Tony, tell our passengers to do something about our escort!" Ozzy ordered. I wasn't sure how to go about that so I opened the door and slipped onto the running board. Cowboy leaned over to hold the door as I worked my head under the canvas covering the back of the truck.

"Hey, put some grenades on those cars or something!" I yelled. Someone shouted back they had it handled. Just then a tree limb hit the door and knocked me off the running board but I managed to hold onto the truck somehow. Cowboy reached out and I took his hand. He pulled me back inside. "Holy shit!" I exclaimed as I slammed the door behind me. Ozzy was howling with laughter. "What's so goddamn funny?" I demanded.

"You could've used the back window," he told me once he regained his composure. I looked back and sure enough, there was a window in the back of the cab. I wasn't sure it was meant to open but I could have broken it if it didn't.

"Why didn't you say something?" I asked.

"I was enjoying the show," Ozzy joked. Cowboy smirked himself.

"Assholes! I almost died out there," I said but I ended up laughing too. Just then, the road behind us went up in a ball of fire and one of the armored cars rolled onto its side. The one behind that had to slow but it was able to get around the disabled car. As I watched the proceedings in my side mirror, Ozzy began to swear. "What?" I asked but I saw the reason for his concern as I turned my attention ahead again. A dead end!

"Fuck this. We're not stopping this time," Ozzy declared. I didn't have time to warn the guys in back so I just held on. The truck burst through the wall of tangled hedgerow and into a field beyond. I was pretty sure something broke because the truck wobbled and shook after we landed. Ozzy took the truck as far as he could across the field, dead ending on the far side where we found another thick hedgerow. God only knows how many of these damn hedgerows there were and what might be on the other side. "Let's disappear!" he said as he climbed out.

"Time to walk you lazy sons a bitches!" Ozzy said to the men in the back of the truck. They piled out of the back, some of them shaking their heads or rubbing their backs after the bumpy ride.

"You drive like an old woman," Bull said as he hopped out.

"Maybe you should have gone with Dusseldorf," Ozzy replied and Bull laughed. We quickly made our way along the hedgerow until we found a way through. We disappeared just as the armored cars came barreling into the field, machine guns blazing. Once through, we ran like mad men. There weren't many roads in the vicinity and the open countryside would take us all the way to Carentan if the map was right. It would also take us right through the German lines if Francois' intelligence was correct.

We finally halted when we ran into a small canal lined with willows. We all fell back against the bank breathing hard. "Everyone have a weapon?" Ozzy asked.

"We're short a couple," Gene replied.

"I've got an extra one and a Lugar too, but I want that back," I offered. Ember and Lech had the MP40's Bull had taken from the guards. I handed the last MP40 to Gene. Ozzy handed his .45 to James and I got to hold on to the Luger, shoving it back into my pants. That couldn't have worked out any better.

"OK, Carentan is only a few miles north, more or less. The Krauts know about us and they are on alert. They've got radios so if we're spotted, the entire Third Reich will be crawling up our asses. We need to keep moving," Ozzy said.

"Thanks for rescuing us once again, mate," James said.

"Thank your man Ember. He's the one that pushed me aside so I could escape," Ozzy said.

"I knew out of all of us you'd be the most likely to pull that off," Ember replied.

"You can buy me a beer in Berlin," Ozzy told the Brits and then asked, "What did you throw out of the truck? That wasn't a grenade."

"No, it was a whole box of them. We found an old ammo box. We filled it with some grenades, pulled the pin on one, closed it up and tossed it out," Gene told us.

"Good thinking," Ozzy said nodding approvingly and then announced, "Let's go home." We all got to our feet and followed Ozzy into the canal and along its bottom, sloshing through the knee deep water.

"What are we doing?" Bull asked the question most of us probably had.

"This will throw the dogs off our trail," James advised us.

We walked several hundred yards crouched low. The German dogs had found where we had entered the canal and more appeared ahead of us. We could see them through the willows with their flashlights but they couldn't see us. Ozzy called a halt to our soggy march.

"They don't know exactly where we are," he whispered and then pointed roughly northwest. We exited the canal quietly and headed for the tree line in the direction Ozzy had indicated. We double-timed it towards the trees and once there, we stopped and watched. Several small groups of soldiers were moving about, flashlights waving this way and that. For the moment, they had lost us and our scent. Their dogs hadn't found our trail yet and if we were lucky, it might be a while before they did.

"We need to keep moving," James assessed.

"I agree. Carentan can't be far. But is that where they expect us to go?" Ozzy wondered.

"Maybe they don't expect us to head directly home," Gene countered.

"So possibly that's just what we should do?" James asked.

"Maybe. I don't know. Either way we've got Krauts behind us and in front," Gene answered.

"Well, we've got to do something. We can't sit here and discuss it all night," Ozzy said and it got quiet. For the first time in days, I could hear the larger war. I suppose I could always hear it, artillery, gunfire, explosions, but I'd gotten used to it. It sounded closer now, however. We were so close but at the same time so far away. After the bridge, we didn't really have a choice any longer. Going back to the safe house would have been as hard as this was. Then I remembered Jimmy.

"Did they get Jimmy?" I asked of no one in particular.

"Afraid so, laddie. Shot him right through the chest. He was dead before he hit the ground," Ember answered.

"Bastards," Bull said. Cowboy shook his head. Bull, Cowboy and I saw him go down before Ember told us to run. I assumed they killed him but I wasn't sure.

"Let's get home and then we can get some payback," Ozzy said. There wasn't much else we could do. "I say we make straight north. We'll run into Carentan or Allied troops near it," Ozzy said. Everyone agreed and we moved out once again. The German search teams were still moving about trying to pick up our trail. It was only a couple of minutes after we pushed through the trees that we heard shouts and dogs barking. They'd found our scent.

"Get moving. This is when running up Currahee will save our asses," Ozzy told us. The Brits probably didn't know what that meant. I was sure Lech didn't. But the five remaining men of Baker Company did. Three miles up and three miles back. We'd run that damn mountain so many times and come to hate it. But we wore it like a badge of honor and hopefully that sacrifice would serve us now.

The eight of us ran as hard as we could, our gear rattling and jangling as we went. We must have run a half mile and through several patches of brush and trees when the first bullets whizzed overhead. We ignored them but obviously we'd been spotted. As far as I was concerned, I was going to run all the way to Carentan but the Krauts had other ideas.

"Jerry on the right," James shouted. A dozen men appeared from out of a hedgerow and began to fire at us. Bullets hit the ground at our feet and buzzed between us.

"This way!" Ozzy yelled and angled left. There was a hedgerow with a single tree growing up from the middle. The tree was huge and must have been hundreds of years old. We headed straight for it. Then a bullet hit Gene and he went down and rolled. Lech and James, didn't miss a step as they grabbed his suspenders and dragged him along. We reached the relative safety of the hedgerow and took cover behind that big tree.

"Where are you hit?" James asked. Gene was grunting.

"Right leg," he groaned.

"We got this. The rest of you defend the position," Ozzy told us. Cowboy, Lech and I took the left side of the big tree. Ember and Bull took the right. I couldn't believe it. The sky was already light to the east. How could it be morning already?

"Two o'clock!" Ember shouted. I saw them now but Cowboy was already lining up a shot. He fired and one of the men went down. Not bad for only having the Kraut gun. The Germans hit the ground and returned fire. We traded lead with them, neither group doing much but keeping the other pinned down. "Watch your ammo! Only shoot what you can hit," Ember told us.

He was right. We had a fair amount of Kraut ammo but who knew how long this might go on. Gene was still writhing on the ground behind the big tree as James and Ozzy worked on him. Suddenly, another group of Krauts appeared from where we had come. They kept their distance as they witnessed the fire fight and set up the MG42 they were carrying. Within moments, that thing was sending even bigger chunks of lead our way.

"Cowboy!" I shouted.

"I can't hit them with this thing. Not at that range," he shouted back. All we could do now was turn and head north again but not with Gene wounded. I looked back and Ozzy was wrapping his leg with a bandage.

"You'll be OK, Gene, but we need to go. You've got to dig deep," Ozzy said.

"I can do it," Gene said as Ozzy and James got him to his feet. Gene almost went down when he put weight on the leg, but they steadied him. Another test and this time Gene grimaced but the pain wasn't so much of shock.

"Ember, Cowboy, you two gents hold them off while the rest of us get a head start. Then follow us. Don't dally long," James said as Ozzy and Gene were already moving. Bull and I, along with Lech, emptied our magazines and then turned to catch up as we reloaded. A few seconds later, Ember and Cowboy did the same. By the time they caught us, we were a hundred yards away and then we all saw it. It was a couple of miles away, but it was unmistakable. The gray structures of Carentan lay ahead, revealed in the light of the coming dawn.

The sight made Gene move just a little faster but we were running out of darkness. Once the sun was up we'd be easy to spot and even easier to kill. "There!" Cowboy called out and pointed off to the left. Across a flooded field stood a small building amongst a stand of trees.

"It will have to do," Ozzy replied and took us that direction. We went right through that flooded field as fast as we could manage. For the time being, the Krauts hadn't caught up to us yet. Long, unbearable seconds passed as we dashed through the water, utterly exposed in the growing light. If they saw us, that building ahead wouldn't be a haven. It would likely be a slaughterhouse.

Gene went down, his leg giving out. Bull tossed me his gun and threw Gene over his shoulder, hardly missing a step. Finally, we made it across, piled into the old shed and looked back from where we'd come. No one followed. We'd made it. Gene was fighting to stay conscious as Ozzy looked him over.

"Fuck, it hurts," Gene moaned.

"We can rest a while. I can give you morphine," Ozzy offered.

"No! No, I'll make it. Maybe a cigarette," Gene replied. He didn't smoke but war had a way of making men turn to vices for comfort.

"Here," I said, handing him one and then lighting it with my Zippo. Gene relaxed almost instantly as he sucked the smoke into his lungs like he'd been smoking his whole life. I don't know why, but those damn Lucky Strikes were like a little piece of heaven. They made everything better.

"Jerry!" Ember whispered suddenly. This little building, an old storage shed or something, was rickety and falling apart so we could see out in every direction even though it had no windows.

"Stay quiet, don't move. Don't shoot unless they come through that door," Ozzy whispered. We all did as he ordered, each of us checking ammo. I took my last pineapple grenade and laid it next to me, just in case. The sun reached across the flooded field but the Germans didn't seem to want to get their feet wet. They were working their way around it instead. It wouldn't be dark again for fifteen or sixteen hours. That was a long time to hide out in this old shed considering it was the only obvious hiding place in the area. Maybe they would assume we weren't stupid enough to choose it and pass us by. Yeah, right!

We watched as the Germans meticulously searched the area. It was only a matter of time before they wound up finding us. I was at a loss as to what we could do to escape. No one else was offering up any ideas either. "Maybe they'll pass us by," I said to no one in particular still hoping against hope.

"Yeah, they'll pass the only obvious structure in sight because we'd never hide in here, right?" Bull replied. I turned to look at him, sure he was being a smart-ass but his face told me he was as worried as I was. "Fuck! Krauts!" Bull whispered suddenly. We all tensed and went quiet. Three of the bastards walked right in front of me, peering into the dark interior through the gaps in the walls of the shed as they did, weapons pointed warily towards us. They found the door on the far side and they had themselves a little conversation. I would have liked to believe they were talking about moving on but I knew they weren't.

The other squad of Germans was hurrying to join them. We all made ready to fight our way out. I had no idea what would happen when they opened that door but I for one wasn't going to die here. I checked my ammo again and picked up the grenade. I looked at Ozzy and he stared back at me. His eyes were hard and full of determination. The other Germans had joined the two outside and then they moved to surround the shed.

Then Lech stood up and went to the door. No one moved to stop him though. No one could believe he was doing it. Finally, Ozzy grabbed the leg of his trousers. Lech looked down and shook his head at Ozzy. Ozzy let go. I had no idea what he was up to. Was he lying to us this whole time? What was he doing? Then Lech opened the door and walked out, greeting the Krauts like he'd known them his whole life as the Germans pointed their weapons at the Pole.

They conversed in German for a bit. Suddenly, the nervous Germans were relaxed and friendly. Lech led them away, past the shed and off into the trees. As they went, Lech turned and winked at us. "Get ready. I think we're leaving," Ozzy said. He helped Gene to his feet and Gene tested his leg. It seemed to take Gene's weight better than it had before. I slipped my grenade back onto my suspenders and then the trees behind us erupted with gunfire.

"That's us," Ozzy said and he threw the door open and we piled out of the shed. We went round to retrieve Lech but found him bleeding from the gut next to five dead Krauts. "Fuck!" Ozzy cursed as he knelt next to Lech.

"Go! I will stay here and send the Nazis in the other direction when they come. They will be here soon. They will assume you killed these men," Lech said, his voice breaking.

"No, you can make it," Ozzy assured him, but Lech was already turning pale.

"I can't. I am already dead. Dead inside. My home, my family, my whole life is gone. Please, leave me," Lech pleaded. He was captured in Poland by the Soviets, then again by the Germans on the eastern front. He'd been pressed into service by the Nazis and sent here to defend against an invasion. He was sure his family was already dead. I stared at Lech and felt completely helpless. I barely knew the man but I liked him. Then we heard shouts off in the distance. "Go!" Lech told us.

"Yeah, I'm sorry. You're a good man. It's been an honor," Ozzy told the Polish man and then shook his hand. Lech looked around and nodded to each of us, his eyes appreciative of our camaraderie. I nodded back. "Let's go," Ozzy ordered. We took off, staying low and within cover when we could. I looked back but Lech wasn't watching us go. He had turned the other direction but whether it was to face the coming German soldiers or to avoid watching us leave, I couldn't know.

Lech's sacrifice must have paid off, however. We weren't followed and when we did finally find good cover we stopped to take some water and let Gene rest his leg. We didn't see any sign of the Krauts. I couldn't help but wonder if Lech was still alive. Would they render aid to what looked like a fellow soldier? Would they take him prisoner again? I had no idea and there was no way I could ever find out. I put it out of my mind and tried to concentrate on making his death, if that was his fate, mean something. If we could get out of here and help defeat Hitler and the Nazis that would make him happy, dead or alive.

"We can't be more than a mile from Carentan," James observed.

"No, we're close. Damn close. I'd prefer to wait and push through tonight but I don't think we could last that long. They're still looking for us," Ozzy said.

"I agree. Send two men ahead to scout. Then we can formulate a plan and do this or die trying," James suggested. It still wasn't an order though he outranked Ozzy.

"Good idea," Ozzy replied and then pointed to me and Cowboy. Why was it always us? "Don't get caught and don't get killed. Just find out what's ahead and find us a way home," Ozzy told us. We both nodded and then Cowboy and I took off, north towards where we needed to be. It wasn't long before we ran into Krauts again. Lots of them but they looked to be pulling out. We didn't know it but in the last day or so, they had gotten their asses kicked just outside of Carentan by the 101st and the 2nd Armored Division. The Battle of Bloody Gulch they came to call it.

"Are they retreating?" I wondered as we observed.

"I don't know but we ought to be able to move up along there," Cowboy said and pointed off towards some thick trees to our right.

"Yeah, maybe. Let's go," I replied. We returned to the others and reported what we saw.

"Retreating?" Ozzy asked.

"Yeah, sort of. They don't look ready for a fight," I told him.

"OK, let's go," Ozzy said and Cowboy took point as we moved out. We weren't running anymore. Now we were back to following hedgerows and tree lines. We were close, so close that now and then you could see a roof or a steeple through the trees off in the distance. I felt like we might actually make it. It was slow going now and Gene seemed thankful for it. He had a bad limp and was in a lot of pain, but he managed to keep up. When we could, one of us would give him a shoulder to lean on as we walked. However, as time passed, we seemed to be getting no closer to our destination.

The area was a jumble of small ditches, canals, hedgerows and the occasional farmhouse, which we had to avoid just in case it was full of Germans. The morning wore on and as it did, my optimism disappeared with it. The longer we stumbled around out here, the better the chance we'd be discovered and never make it back to where we belonged. Then Ozzy stopped us and we took a break.

"This is like a damned maze. We could wander back

and forth trying to find a safe route to Carentan all day. On the other hand, if we just head straight there in the open, we'll likely all be killed before we make it," Ozzy said.

"We'll go look around again," Cowboy offered.

"Do it," was all Ozzy said in reply. Again Cowboy and I headed off to see what we could see. This time, however, we got more than we bargained for. Cowboy and I crept up to the edge of a small canal and peered over. Right there, across from us, a Kraut stood taking a leak. He looked up and then did a double take as he realized what he was seeing. He zipped up quickly and turned to run. Cowboy drew his revolver, the big pistol he carried back home, but I pushed it down.

"They'll hear," I said.

"But he's going to tell them anyway," Cowboy countered. But it was too late. The German soldier was shouting. Moments later, bullets flew our way and a grenade fell into the canal just off to our right. We both ducked as it went off and covered us in water and mud. "Fuck!" Cowboy yelled. Now he had his MP40 up and ready. "I'll cover you. See how many there are," he told me.

"Why don't I cover you and you poke your head up and see?" I replied sarcastically.

"Because, it was my idea," he advised me. I scowled back at my friend as the odd bullet sailed over us.

"Fuck!" was all I said and then pointed with my thumb over the canal's bank. Cowboy crept up and raised his gun and sprayed bullets beyond. I popped my head up and sank back down quickly, my stomach sinking right along with me.

"What?" he asked me.

"There must be a hundred fucking Germans," I said. Then suddenly, Ozzy slid in between us.

"What the fuck? I didn't tell you to start a fucking war over here," Ozzy admonished us and then smiled devilishly. Bullets whizzed over our heads and another grenade hit the bank of the canal and then spun off sideways. We covered up as it went off, covering us in dirt, gravel and dead grass, but not much else. The rest of our dwindling group joined us, throwing themselves on the embankment.

"There must be a hundred fucking Krauts over there," Bull observed.

"Thanks. You're master of the obvious," Ozzy replied. Bull rolled his eyes.

"Well, we're in the thick of it now," James observed as he fired across the embankment. Why the Germans didn't just come over and kill us, I wasn't sure. Ozzy knew, however.

"They think we're attacking in force," he informed us. Just then, a couple of MG42s began firing on the ditch but they were way off target, or maybe they just figured there were more of us to hit spread out along the ditch.

"Then we should use that mistaken assumption to our advantage," Ember added. Ozzy gestured for us to move.

"He's right. Spread out. Make them think we're a larger force. Keep moving...that way," Ozzy ordered and pointed in the general direction of Carentan. We did as he wanted, firing over the small canal as we went. Only Gene was lying down. The rest of us were crouched low, firing shots over the canal and then moving a few yards and doing it again. It must have worked because the German's fired all along the length of the ditch, their fire spread out and seemingly random.

Moving towards Carentan sounded like a fine idea. We kept moving towards our objective, keeping the Germans pinned down so they couldn't figure out they faced only seven men. Unfortunately, we ran out of ditch to use as cover as it went into a culvert that flowed under a road. "This is it," I said as Cowboy and I reached the end of the line. I doubted Ozzy thought we could make it all the way to Carentan or the American lines like this so he must've had another idea. He always did. Cowboy and I looked at him expectantly.

"I'm out of ideas," Ozzy said. That wasn't what I was hoping for him to say. The Germans couldn't get at us directly and as long as they thought we were a bigger force and they didn't seem prepared to advance to find out otherwise. Still, this ruse wasn't going to last forever. We we're going to have to fight our way out or die within sight of Carentan.

"We can take our chances and retreat," James offered.

"We might have too. That road is too wide and to open to cross. Those MGs would tear us to pieces," Ozzy told all of us as much as James. They were spraying random fire along the bank still but when we popped up to cross the road they would quickly turn on us and cut us down.

"What about that culvert?" Ember suggested. Ozzy looked hopeful. He popped his head up over the bank and looked down into it, then slipped right back down behind it as several bullets hit near him. If I had done that, I'd be dead.

"Yeah, Cowboy, lover boy, cover us. Once we're down in the ditch and moving, you follow," Ozzy said and winked at me. Why did I get the feeling he was enjoying this somehow. Now the entire company of Germans was engaged. Some were still firing on our original position some even further down along the canal. But most of the fire was directed right at us as they began to figure out no one was returning fire from the other positions. I turned to Cowboy and he nodded at me as we loaded fresh magazines into our weapons. Ozzy grabbed Gene and made ready. Cowboy and I popped up and fired.

As we did, the other five men rolled into the ditch and began scrambling down its length as we provided suppressing fire. Once past us, they filed into the culvert one by one. Bull barely fit. Cowboy and I emptied our magazines and threw ourselves over the embankment. Both of us were hit as we did. I had a bullet take off the toe of my boot but Cowboy took one in the arm.

"You OK?" I asked as we crawled along.

"Yeah, I'll live," he grunted from just ahead of me. We crawled on our bellies through the mud and shallow water as fast as we could. I couldn't help but imagine the German's knew what was going on and they'd appear along the ditch and kill both of us before we made it to the culvert. But before I could finish the thought, I heard Ozzy and the others begin to return fire from the other side of the road. Finally, I was in the culvert and safe for the time being. Just ahead of me, Cowboy struggled to wiggle though the small pipe. How the hell did Bull get through here?

Cowboy crawled out and I was right behind him. We emerged to find the other five men firing in all directions. "While you two were making out down there in the tunnel of love, twenty Krauts crossed the road and flanked us," Ozzy explained as Cowboy and I began to lay down fire.

Now we were pinned down in a ditch, willows behind us and the road the only real cover we had. I was pretty sure the Germans had figured out we weren't a larger force as another twenty crossed the road in plain sight. Then I saw him. Field Marshall Von Dusseldorf rode atop a fucking Kraut tank and began shouting orders as it crawled towards us. The tank's turret slowly turned our way.

"Fuck! Get down," Ozzy shouted. We all took cover behind the road in the small ditch as the tank fired. A shell roared over our heads and exploded behind us. Then we heard more tracks behind us. We all looked as the trees shook and were mowed down as a whole bunch of armor was headed our way. This was it. There was no escaping now. "I am not going to fucking surrender this close to our objective," Ozzy swore and slapped another magazine into his machine pistol. Then one of the approaching tanks crashed out of the trees behind us.

"That's not a Kraut tank. That's a fucking Sherman!" Bull shouted. Its cannon erupted with smoke and fire just as a second and then a third tank broke through the trees. Each of those let loose and the field beyond exploded with fire and death. Men, dozens of them, came through the trees beyond as the Sherman tanks stopped to seek out other targets. The seven of us cheered and hugged one another as men wearing the screaming eagle patch of the 101st Airborne surrounded us and began picking off Germans.

The German Panzer carrying the Field Marshal was backing up quickly and one of the Sherman tanks just missed it. Cowboy stood up and grabbed the nearest man. "Hey, let me borrow your rifle," Cowboy said to him. The guy looked at him funny but handed it over anyway. Cowboy ran across the road and fell to one knee. I had no idea what he was doing until he shouldered the rifle. He was aiming at Dusseldorf.

"Get him, Cowboy," Ozzy shouted. Cowboy lined up and I saw him exhale. A moment later, he pulled the trigger. We all watched, that split second seemed like an eternity. It had to be three hundred yards but Cowboy probably would have killed the Field Marshall if the Sherman behind us didn't beat him to the punch. The Kraut tank exploded in a ball of fire, the turret coming free and landing several yards away. Germans were running for cover and the 101st was thinning their numbers as they went.

"Did you see that?" Cowboy turned and asked.

"The Sherman nailed that sucker!" I replied.

"No, not that. I killed the ol' Field Marshal," Cowboy replied excitedly.

"The hell you did. The Sherman got him," Bull argued and winked at me.

"Bullshit! I hit him right in the heart. How did you miss it?" Cowboy said as he wandered back across the road.

"Sorry, didn't see it, Cowboy," I said. Then Ozzy came up behind me.

"Did you even shoot? I couldn't tell with that tank

firing," Ozzy said. I looked back and he had that wry smile on his face.

"Assholes!" Cowboy said, shaking his head but he was smiling. We all saw the Field Marshal take Cowboy's bullet in the chest a split second before the tank was destroyed, but we weren't about to let him know that. Then Cowboy suddenly saluted and we turned to find a Lieutenant approaching. He wasn't from our Company but he looked familiar. The rest of us saluted and tried to come to attention, though Gene was having trouble standing.

"At ease. What are you guys doing out here? You were making quite a racket. I wasn't aware of any operations out this way," he asked suspiciously. But then a squad leader from Baker Company joined us.

"Ozzy? Is that you?" Sergeant Overton asked.

"You know these men? What the hell is this all about?" the Lieutenant pressed.

"Yeah, I know them. These guys are supposed to be dead," Sergeant Overton exclaimed.

"Dead? All right, what the fuck is going on?" the Lieutenant reiterated. The two Brits joined us. The fighting was pretty much over, the Germans routed and retreating. We stood on the road, all of us now though Gene was down on one knee looking rather pale. Lieutenant Graham greeted our Lieutenant who then asked as his frustration mounted, "And why are there Brits here?"

"First off, I've got an injured man," Ozzy said.

"No, I can wait. I want to hear this," Gene replied as the Lieutenant sent a man to fetch a medic.

"Fine. Lieutenant, I'm Corporal Oscar Jennings. My men and I escaped a crippled C-47 on D-Day but we ended up about twelve miles south with no way to link up. We've been operating with the assistance of the French resistance ever since. Today, we were finally able to break through but ran into these Kraut troops. Then the armor and these men arrived to assist us," Ozzy said. Assist us? We were about to get our asses handed to us on a silver platter.

"And the British?" the Lieutenant asked. This time James stepped up.

"Excuse me. I'm Lieutenant James Graham, British 6th Airborne. I'm afraid our transport was off course like these yanks. Sergeant Stewart and I were taken prisoner and held south of here. These men rescued us several days past and since we've been assisting them. These men have managed to be quite effective over the last week," James informed his counterpart.

A medic arrived but Gene waived him off. The medic stood by to watch the show. The Lieutenant looked skeptical, but a British Lieutenant was telling him the same story Ozzy had. He rubbed his chin as he looked us over. "Let's go see Colonel Sink and sort this out," the Lieutenant said. He turned and found his Jeep and then invited Ozzy and James to ride with him. I guess the rest of us had to walk. Ozzy, at least, helped Gene into the Jeep with him.

"What the fuck is his problem?" I asked after they drove off.

"I don't know. He's got a stick up his ass or something," Bull replied as we started to walk towards Carentan. Along the way, we saw a few Baker Company guys.

"Nice of you boys to show up," one of them said as we approached.

"Fuck you, Jones," I replied and then shook his hand.

"Where you boys been? You missed all the fun," Jones said as he greeted the rest of us.

"Yeah, Tony spent the last week shacking up with some French girl," Bull told him.

"No shit? You guys got any smokes?" Jones asked, taking Bull at his word apparently. Maybe he just didn't care.

"Shut up, Bull," I said and slugged him in the arm but it was like hitting a brick wall. Bull just laughed and

Cowboy joined him. "Where's the CP?" I asked and Jones pointed over his shoulder. As the four of us left, Jones asked one of the other guys, "Who's the limey?" Ember turned and grinned at me as we walked away. We found the command post and Colonel Sink was already there. Ozzy had just finished telling him the story.

"Come in," Colonel Sink said and after we saluted him, he faced Ozzy as he leaned over a table. "So, sounds like you boys have had a time of it. I'd be skeptical if I didn't have some intelligence backing up your story and you didn't have a British Lieutenant with you. So, you engaged the 17th SS, just the six of you?" Sink asked.

"No, Sir. We had help from the French resistance," Ozzy explained.

"Good work, son. I want to see your after action reports by 0900 along with any recommendations for commendations. Lieutenant Graham, we'll see about getting you and your man back to your unit. They're east of here, or so I'm led to believe. Things are still a bit...uncertain," Colonel Sink told us. James stepped forward.

"Sir, thank you. Permission to speak?" James asked and Sink told him to go ahead. "Sir, Sergeant Stewart and I are grateful to your men for rescuing us. But beyond that, let me say that these men, including the man we lost, are some of the bravest soldiers I've ever met. Ozzy, excuse me, Corporal Jennings, is a decisive leader and I happily deferred to his judgment. The Americans are lucky to have such men," James told Colonel Sink.

"Thank you. We're pretty proud of them too," Sink replied. James saluted and Colonel Sink saluted back. But Ozzy wasn't finished.

"Colonel, we were forced to leave Sergeant Collins behind with a French farmer when he was injured on D-Day. May we have permission to retrieve him," Ozzy asked. Sink looked at him, frowning.

"Where is he?" Sink asked.

"Sainteny," Ozzy replied. Sink sighed.

"We don't hold that area yet. We've barely secured Carentan. We can't risk it. We'll get him when we take that area. Grab some grub and a hot shower. We're here for a few days at least," Colonel Sink told us. Ozzy saluted and the colonel saluted back. We did as Sink ordered, got some showers, found some food and hot coffee. It wasn't as fancy as the French food but it was familiar and tasted pretty damned good.

As we sat on the steps of some building drinking coffee and unwinding, Lieutenant Graham got up and wandered off without a word. Nobody thought much of it. The rest of us, including Ember, talked about the last week or so. It had been a wild ride. It already seemed like some kind of dream. Ember asked about Jimmy at one point.

"Private James Gonzalez. He was from Chowchilla, California. He was only nineteen. I wasn't too sure about him but he turned out to be a good soldier. Rest in peace, Jimmy," Ozzy told the Scotsman. Most of us echoed that, whispering, "Rest in peace." After that, we sat there on those steps quietly. I don't know about anyone else but I was glad just to be alive and remembering Jimmy drove that point home.

"How's the leg?" Ozzy asked Gene after a few minutes.

"Hurts," he replied.

"You should go to the medical tent and get that looked at," Ozzy replied.

"I wouldn't do that just yet," James said as he walked up suddenly.

"Why not?" Gene asked curiously.

"I suppose you can if you want to miss all the fun. Colonel Sink gave us permission to go get your Sergeant," James announced.

"What? How did you manage that?" Ozzy asked.

"We had a discussion...Sergeant," James replied meaningfully. Ozzy narrowed his eyes as James extended his hand. "Congratulations on your promotion," James said.

"What did you tell Sink?" Ozzy asked.

"Ah, well. Nothing that didn't need saying," James replied being cagey. Ozzy shook his hand and then the rest of us congratulated him as well.

"Thanks...for whatever," Ozzy told the Brit.

"You're welcome, mate. I owe you my life...twice. So, it seems Colonel Sink needs a few men to go on patrol south of here. See what's up, gather intelligence, usual stuff," James told us.

"You're not bad...for a Brit," Ozzy said and then told us what we needed to do. We spent the rest of the day catching some shut eye, gathering some new weapons, M1 Garands, Thompsons, pineapple grenades and plenty of ammo. We kept the Kraut weapons for souvenirs, however. Gene got his leg bandaged up but he refused to go back to the beaches to a real aid station or, God forbid, a hospital ship. Nothing was broken and though it hurt, Gene was more than happy to tough it out. My toes were intact and Cowboy's arm wasn't much more than a scratch.

We had barely made our way to Carentan and the relative safety that came with it but now we were going to go right back where we started. We must've been crazy. I never found out what James told Colonel Sink to convince him to let us go, but I'm glad he did. I couldn't help but wonder if I might see Margaux. We'd been living behind enemy lines for a week. What was another few hours?

We left at dusk, just the seven of us. Ozzy, Gene, Bull, Cowboy and I were the only men left from the C-47 that went down on D-Day. Lieutenant Graham and Sergeant Stewart would be with us for a while until things settled down and they could make it back to their units. As we picked our way through the hedgerows and the groves of trees south of Carentan, it struck me how normal it felt. Carentan with all its relative comforts was what seemed unusual after a week of French food, not to mention the companionship, and sneaking around the French countryside. In retrospect, those comforts were going to be few and far between for the 101st as the war dragged on.

We had about seven miles to cover but the Germans had been beat pretty bad a day or so earlier. They had pulled back and were attempting to gather strength. We never saw so much as a patrol on the way to Claude's farmhouse. But as we approached Sainteny, we saw something else. "Is that ours?" Cowboy asked as we closed on the twisted metal that was once a C-47.

"I think so," Ozzy replied. Gene bowed his head. I said a quiet prayer.

"Nasty business this war," James offered.

"Should we gather dog tags?" I asked.

"No, we'll let them know the location back at headquarters. It's too dangerous to spend much time here," Ozzy told me. I guess he was right. We took a moment longer to stare at the burned out carcass of the plane that carried us across the English Channel and took the lives of so many men down with it and then we moved on. Soon, things started to look familiar.

"Shit, we landed right over there," Bull said. Cowboy was on point and he led us right to the ditch we found ourselves in on D-Day. Sainteny was just beyond as was the sign post Cowboy and I had ventured out to read that first night. We carefully crept out of the ditch and then towards the farmhouse where we'd left Sarge that first night in Normandy. Ozzy sent Cowboy and I to knock on the back door just like I had before. The only difference was Cowboy was watching my back and I was with Jimmy then. It was a strange feeling.

I knocked just like I had on D-Day and just like that night, a light shone through heavy curtains in the window next to the door. Claude cautiously opened the door and stared at me, his eyes full of disbelief.

"Tony?" Claude asked.

"Yeah. How you doing, Claude?" I replied.

"Come in, come in," he told me. I told Cowboy to wait as I went inside the house.

"We've come to get Sarge," I told Claude. He frowned.

"He's no longer here," Claude said and he must have seen the look on my face. "No, he's well. Francois and his daughter came to take him to safety this morning. He is with them," Claude explained.

"Oh, you scared me. Do you know where they went?" I asked.

"To Francois' home. It is just down the road. He has a secret place in his cellar so Stanley will be safe," Claude told me. Stanley? I never heard him called that before. That was his name, Stanley Collins, but I'd always just called him Sarge.

"Which way?" I asked eagerly.

"That way," Claude said and pointed, "There is a path behind my house. Take that and you will not be seen." I shook Claude's hand.

"Thank you. Stay safe," I told him and went for the door.

"No, thank you and the others. God bless you all," Claude said. I turned and nodded before I left and took Cowboy back to the others.

"He's down the road with friends," I whispered.

"Your girl?" Ozzy asked as much as stated.

"I hope so!" I said and then told them all to follow me. We found the path through the woods behind Claude's house. It was just wide enough to walk single file, trees and brush arched overhead. The Krauts would never see us in there. We followed the path for a hundred yards or so until we found another house. As was usual, no lights were on. I just hoped Francois and Margo were there.

"Tony, do the honors," Ozzy said as everyone crouched and waited. I approached the house and looked it over. No signs of life but that didn't mean much. Lights drew allied aircraft but Francois and Margaux were with the resistance. They probably didn't want any kind of unwanted attention. I found the back door and knocked quietly. I waited but no one appeared. My heart sank. I checked the far side of the house but when I turned to go report to Ozzy that no one was home, a shadowy figure peeled away from the wall and pointed a gun at me.

"Margaux?" I asked. The gun lowered and then fell to the ground and Margaux jumped into my arms.

"Tony? Why are you here?" she asked.

"You don't want to see me?" I teased her.

"Stop it. What are you doing here?" she asked again. I gave her the short version of our journey since we had parted and why we had come. "Stanley is safe. Come, come. Are you alone?" she replied.

"No," I informed her. We gathered the others and Margo led us to the cellar entrance at the back of the house. She opened the door and she led us down inside. Francois held a rifle pointed at us and for a moment his eyes were full of confusion.

"We have visitors," Margaux told her father. Francois stood and smiled walking directly to Ozzy.

"My friend. What brings you back to us so soon?" Francois asked.

"Just out for a stroll. We figured we'd take Sarge back with us," Ozzy said. Just then, Sergeant Collins emerged from behind a row of shelves.

"What if I don't want to go back? Chow's good, clean sheets, pretty girls," Sarge said. He was on makeshift crutches and dressed in civilian clothes.

"How's the leg?" Ozzy asked.

"It's still there," he replied and then came over to the Brits and shook their hands. "These two told me all about your little adventures. I'm proud of you guys. You did the right thing," Sarge told us. Everyone gathered around and greeted him but Margaux pulled me aside.

"How long will you be here?" she asked. I sighed because I saw the look in her eye. French girls!

"We have to go right back," I told her. She frowned and then kissed me. Not like before either. This was a real kiss. I grabbed her and pulled her close. God, I wanted to do so much more.

"Geez, he's doing it again, Ozzy," Bull informed the group. Everyone laughed.

"Francois, you didn't tell me about that," Sarge said.

"I'm afraid he's going to steal my daughter," Francois replied. Margaux broke the kiss and looked past me at her father, smiling at him. Francois winked at her.

"Sorry, I got carried away," I announced.

"No, take your time. The war will wait," Ozzy said making me laugh. "Can you travel?" Ozzy asked Sarge.

"Slowly. I'm afraid I'll just slow you down. We're still behind the lines, aren't we?" Sarge asked.

"You know, you're in good hands. Maybe you should stay," Ozzy offered.

"The doctor says his leg will heal. We can keep him safe here," Francois told us.

"Twist my arm. I'm glad you guys came to check on me but I don't want to be a liability. I don't want to get anyone killed because I can't walk," Sarge said.

"We probably won't see you again, Sarge. I think that's a ticket home," Gene told him. Sarge nodded solemnly.

"You're probably right. It was an honor to serve with you guys. Even if it was just for five minutes once we hit the ground. I'm looking forward to going home but part of me wishes I was staying. I'll miss you guys. Ozzy, I'll put in a word for you once I'm picked up by someone. You should take my place," Sarge said.

"I already have, I think. Sink promoted me this morning," Ozzy replied.

"Wise man. I feel even better knowing these boys are in good hands. By the way, where's Jimmy? He didn't make it, did he?" Sarge asked, but he knew. Ozzy shook his head and Margaux looked at me.

"I'm sorry," she said.

"Lech didn't make it either," I told her. Margaux shook her head.

"I'm glad you made it back. You must take care of yourself," she told me. It was almost an order.

"I'm going to come back and marry you so I guess I don't have a choice," I said.

"No you don't," she replied sternly. The others were already saying their goodbyes. This time it was less desperate and we lingered a while. Ozzy ended up telling Francois, Sarge and Margaux about our journey to Carentan. Margaux had a mix of horror and admiration on her face as she held on to my arm while we listened.

"I'm afraid you've got a lot more adventures ahead. I pray this is done quickly," Sarge told us. So did we but it wasn't to be. After Sarge wished us well, we all said our final goodbyes. Leaving Margaux was getting harder and harder. Ozzy was nearly forced to drag me away.

"Come on, lover boy. Time to go to work," he told me as he pulled me out of Margaux's arms.

"I love you, Tony," Margaux told me and then blew me a kiss.

"I love you too," I said and then we were gone. I refused to look back as we made our way down the path to Claude's house and then back the way we had come. We almost ran into one patrol but the lines were broken, less defined after the battle in Carentan. We slipped through easily now. I wondered why we hadn't tried earlier to make it back but I knew. The Germans had fortified positions between where we had landed and the beaches. The Atlantic Wall had been breached, however, and though we'd take some steps backwards over the next ten months, the German's had essentially lost the war when we secured the beachheads.

We made it back to Carentan without incident. Gene was in a lot of pain but he still refused to submit to the doctors. He didn't want to be pulled out of action.

Corporal Eugene S. Rosenberg was eventually given a battlefield commission of Sergeant but he was killed at Bastogne in his foxhole. He killed a lot of Germans before he died, however, so he didn't die in vain. Still, his death hit us hard.

Gene was the only one besides Jimmy that didn't make it home but he wasn't the only casualty. Cowboy was hit by a sniper during Operation Market Garden and he was laid up in the hospital for a while but he managed to escape and join us before the Battle of the Bulge. I carried his big revolver while he was gone and gave it back to him when he returned. Walter W. McCloud went back to Nevada after the war and lived out his life as a real cowboy. He got married, had three daughters and died in 1997.

Bull was wounded later that summer but it wasn't bad. He took some shrapnel in his ass. He got hit again in Bastogne and that earned him a ticket back to England. He recovered and went back home to Norman, OK. After he lost his house in a tornado, he moved to Arizona where he became a firefighter. He died in the line of duty in 1973 when a roof collapsed. John P. Tucker was trying to save another firefighter when he died. That's the way Bull was. He left behind a widow and an adult son. He was only months from retirement.

The two Brits made it back to their unit about a week after we returned to Carentan. Lieutenant James Graham was killed in action in August 1944. I was told by Ember when I looked him up on a trip to Europe many years after the war. Lieutenant Embry Stewart fought till the end of the war and returned home to Scotland afterwards. He's still alive as is his wife and they have three children, eight grand kids and several great grand kids. We still speak occasionally by phone.

Me, well, I never was seriously wounded. Nothing I'd let them pull me off the lines for anyway. In May 1945, I made it back to France and made good on my promise. I married Margaux in a small church in Sainteny. Ozzy was there as was Francois, Claude and some extended family. My mom got over it eventually. She didn't mind that Margaux wasn't Italian but it took her years to forgive her baby boy for not inviting her to the wedding. Margaux came to the United States with me when they finally let me out of the Army but we visited France often over the years.

We had two children, Tony Jr. and Monique. We named our daughter after Margaux's mother. Margaux died in 2004. I buried her next to Francois in Normandy. I miss her so. When I finally go, that's where I'll be buried. My heart has always been in that place. That week in Normandy changed my life. I met my wife there and made friendships that endured long after the war ended. The most special was Oscar P. Jennings but I always knew him as Ozzy.

Ozzy was never wounded during the war. He stayed in the Army after the German's were defeated and fought in Korea too. He came through two wars without a scratch. He retired a Captain with a chest full of medals and ribbons. Even though I never made it past Corporal, Ozzy and I formed a friendship that lasted our entire lives. Ozzy lived in his hometown of Wautoma, Wisconsin until his death in 2007. His wife died a month later. Their five children and most of their grandchildren helped me spread his ashes in the lake where he loved to fish.

D-Day was a long time ago. Sometimes it feels like it was all a dream. Other times it seems like it was yesterday. I'm all that's left of the men of Baker Company. The six of us that found ourselves lost in France but chose to do what we could. Jimmy never made it out of there. Gene never made it home either. The rest have died along the way. Even Margaux is gone now. I find myself longing for those times again and the companionship of those I served with and met along the way.

I'm one of the last. Soon, there will be nobody left that

fought in that war or even lived through it. If I had one wish, it would be that the sacrifices made, the lives lost and changed forever, the unimaginable destruction will never be forgotten. I wouldn't trade my time in France for the world but I sometimes feel selfish for that. So many paid a cost that can never be calculated and I hope I've lived my life in a way that honors their memory. If God is smiling down upon me, soon I'll be able to ask them myself, standing humbly before them all.

APPENDIX

Baker Company was originally published as a four part serial. It has been my biggest success to date, selling thousands of copies of both the individual episodes and the "Box Set," both in ebook format. However, many people have asked about a paperback edition since they don't read electronic books. Well, here it is.

What follows are the notes about each episode that I included in the original ebooks. They give some insight into their development and the history surrounding the story. Enjoy!

EPISODE 1

Baker Company sprang from an idea for a web comic that never came to fruition. When I began writing, I decided to adapt that idea into serialized fiction. I like the idea of serials, like television episodes or old movie serials such as Flash Gordon. Many people don't realize that serialized fiction is how stories were delivered in the 1800's. Charles Dickens made a name for himself writing serialized fiction, including David Copperfield.

This particular story seemed perfect for this publishing

model. The story spanned a relatively long period of time, had several disparate events and the serial model fits the era. Baker Company is my homage to the bravery and sacrifice displayed during World War II. I'm a WW2 buff and the Normandy invasion is one of my favorite campaigns to study. That's why I've chosen D-Day and the weeks afterwards as the setting for my story.

I chose to follow the exploits of a fictionalized group of men instead of trying to tell the story of actual persons. The men of Baker Company and the other characters are meant to represent all the men and women that fought fascism and tyranny in Europe and all around the globe. The story is also to entertain. It is fiction and has an adventure aspect to it but it also has enough realism to give readers a small taste of what really happened. The purpose is not to glorify war but glorify the men that were forced to fight it.

Baker Company is not the naked heroism of John Wayne movies. This serial hints at the darker side of war, the sacrifice and the unique camaraderie developed amongst men in dire circumstances. Yes, the Germans have the aim of the Stormtroopers in Star Wars, but this is historical fiction after all. Real war is far from entertaining, but the themes and actions within that can be. I hope everyone that reads this enjoys the romance and adventure but also understands there is something deeper.

EPISODE 2

Episode 2 of Baker Company is your typical middle chapter. It continues the story, adds a few characters and sets up the ending of the story. Still Episode 2 is a complete story with a beginning and an end. You won't find out how the characters got into the situation they find themselves in, but the story is still satisfying (though I do recommend you read Episode 1). It also contains elements and storylines that continue throughout the series, namely the budding romance between Tony and Margaux.

The new characters are designed to accomplish two things. One, they help give the men of Baker Company some support, which they need. Two, they are designed to illustrate other aspects of the war. The invasion of Normandy wasn't just an American operation. British, Canadian and free French, among others, participated. So, the men of Baker Company have the opportunity to rescue a couple of British paratroopers that have been captured.

On the other side, largely forgotten, the Nazis utilized captured troops, mainly from the Eastern front, to help defend the Atlantic wall. Many died during the landings and the subsequent battles but they have largely been forgotten. With that in mind, I've added an Ostlegionen (Eastern soldier) character. In this case, he is Polish and his story illustrates another forgotten event, the invasion of Poland by the Russians prior to the German invasion.

World War II was a huge event in human history. Over seventy million people died during the conflict, most of them civilians. I hope the little stories, such as Gene's Jewish background, Margaux's mother and the Polish soldier's tale, give readers a hint of the wider war beyond the stuff we focus on, namely the war after 1941 in the Pacific and after D-Day. There was so much more and the effects of World War II will ripple through history for centuries.

EPISODE 3

Episode 3 is just the beginning of the end. It's a shameless cliffhanger is classic serial style. Just when things look like they might work out it all goes to hell. After some adventures and introducing the whole cast in the first two episodes, Episode 3 sets up the ending while telling a story all by itself.

The bridge was always part of the plan. In fact, at one point the bridge was the major set piece in a single story and at one time was planned for an earlier episode. But I needed some warm bodies to hold the bridge and the Brits and Lech provide some more firepower. But even that wasn't enough.

In all the episodes so far, some bit of good luck or fortune saves the day. It's not realistic for such a small force to really fight effectively against so many Germans. In this episode, the day is saved by the US Army Air Forces in dramatic fashion. It makes me want to write something about the air war over Europe.

We also loose a character in Episode 3. It had to happen. That's part of war and not to show that aspect would be cheating in a way. This death won't be the last in the serial or during the war beyond for our little band. It was tough to choose who would die but one is senseless as so many during war are. The other makes more sense but it's still a sad event.

Now, with only one episode to go, the story will become smaller, so to speak. From big, exciting operations with dramatic endings, the story becomes a dash for safety. Don't worry, the fourth episode has its excitement and drama but it's more personal. We'll also get a satisfying ending that ties up the loose ends. It's not a happily ever after, the war still rages after all, but we will get a glimpse of the future.

EPISODE 4

In Episode 4, the finale, the action picks up right where we left off in Episode 3. What's a serial without a good old fashioned cliff hanger anyway? While the cliffhanger is resolved quickly, our heroes find themselves deeper in trouble as they get closer to their goal, Carentan. If I've done my job, you won't see how the men of Baker Company can ever escape.

Of course, they do and then all that's left is the epilogue. I'd been considering exactly how to handle the end since I began this serial. I knew I needed to provide some closure and let the reader know how things turned out once the story was finished. Being that the episodes are narrated in the first person by Tony, it seemed only right that he tell the story after the story. I think he did a fine job.

We've also found a new villain, though we never know him by any other name that Field Marshal von Dusseldorf, the name Ozzy gives him jokingly when they first encounter the man. He finally puts a face to the Nazis and becomes a focal point for the heroes. He's not running around chewing on the scenery, taking over the whole show, but we get to see enough of his arrogance to dislike the man.

We also lose some characters, it is war after all, and we learn of more loses in the epilogue. All in all, we get a happy for now ending with a hint that some characters do in fact live happily ever after. The ending is bittersweet, both for the men of Baker Company and for me. I'll miss these guys. They've been a part of my life for over a year and a big part over this past summer. I'm proud of the work and thankful I've reached so many readers. Thank you all and I look forward to entertaining you in the future.

Finally, I'd just like to say a word of thanks to the men and women that sacrificed so much during those times and offer this serial as a tribute. I'd also like to remember the innocents that suffered and died at the hands of tyranny and oppression. It is in their memory that we can find answers in our difficult and complicated world and avoid the same mistakes. All we have to do is choose to see.

ABOUT THE AUTHOR

Dan McMartin is a retired engineer turned writer. Dan enjoys writing World War II fiction, fantasy and other men's fiction. Beyond writing, Dan enjoys fly fishing, Jeeps and the outdoors. He lives in Nevada with his family.

Visit Dan at his website: **flyfishnevada.com**

This is a work of fiction. Any similarity to real persons, living or deceased, is unintentional. It is intended as entertainment and some historical liberties were taken. This story is dedicated to the men and women who fought tyranny and especially those that sacrificed their lives in the name of freedom and liberty during World War II.

CPSIA information can be obtained
at www.ICGtesting.com
Printed in the USA
BVOW08s0721090417
480736BV00001B/331/P